Mills & Boon Classics

A chance to read and collect some of the best-loved novels from Mills & Boon – the world's largest publisher of romantic fiction.

Every month, four titles by favourite Mills & Boon authors will be re-published in the *Classics* series.

A list of other titles in the *Classics* series can be found at the end of this book.

Anne Hampson

WIFE FOR A PENNY

MILLS & BOON LIMITED
LONDON · TORONTO

First published 1972
Australian copyright 1979
Philippine copyright 1979
This edition 1979

© Anne Hampson 1972

ISBN 0 263 73176 6

Set in 10 on 12 pt Baskerville

*Made and printed in Great Britain by
C. Nicholls & Company Ltd.
The Philips Park Press, Manchester*

CHAPTER ONE

'ROLL up, roll up! Don't miss this opportunity of kissing the most beautiful girl in Cheshire! Get your tickets here – only a penny, gentlemen – *one* penny!'

'I'm not,' hissed Elizabeth Dawes through her teeth, 'the most beautiful girl in Cheshire!'

'Roll up, roll up,' grinned the persistent Grace, ignoring Liz's scowl. 'You, sir, aren't you going to speculate a penny?'

He stood by the stall, one of the many stalls on the vast green, his dark eyes roving with lazy disinterest from Grace to the indescribably beautiful girl at her side.

'Kisses in this part of the world appear to be cheap,' he drawled, the hint of a foreign accent enriching the depth and tone of his voice.

'Special offer – one day only,' came the prompt and crisp retort from Grace. 'Such an opportunity will never fall your way again.' What a devastatingly handsome man, she thought – but frowned on making a closer examination. Mouth too thin, eyes hard as steel, jaw flexed. There was an indolent touch to his voice as he said,

'Might I ask which one of you is offering this – er – bargain?'

'How polite you are,' commented Grace with sarcasm.

'Polite, but not short-sighted.' Her tone held no rancour; Grace's popularity was proof enough that what had been denied her in looks was amply compensated for in personality. That personality was sunny and warm; her conversation could be light or deeply intelligent, depending on the requirements of the moment.

5

Those keen dark eyes glinted at her words, and the hard mouth became even more tightly compressed. What nationality was he? Grace wondered. From the East, certainly. Greek, perhaps.

Liz was also debating on his nationality. Dark-skinned, with black hair and grey-green eyes; tall and sinewed and giving the impression of animal-like strength ... a face that could have been etched in stone – severe lines, clear-cut, prominent cheekbones and an aquiline nose. Merciless and formidable, was Liz's ultimate conclusion.

'I'll take a couple,' from a smiling young man who had just strolled up from the stall close by.

A frown crossed Grace's brow; she looked severely at him.

'I'm not sure I want my fiancé kissing my best friend!'

He laughed.

'That's what I like to hear. I like my women to be jealous.' Ray produced his money and received his tickets, although with reluctance from Grace who was still feigning that severity which only served to bring another laugh from him as he moved away to a nearby stall.

'Roll up!' repeated Grace with an eye to business as she saw several young men approaching. 'Don't miss this unique opportunity of kissing the most beautiful girl in Cheshire!'

And there was no doubt that Liz was very lovely. At sixteen she had ridden proudly through the streets of Knutsford, the town with the only 'royal' May Day in the country and, therefore, the town whose May Queen was the most photographed of them all. With her golden head held high and a look of haughty disdain for her wide-eyed 'subjects' lining the streets, Liz had indeed appeared most regal.

6

'Beautiful, but heartless; you can see it in her face,' was a comment often repeated as she went on her triumphant way to the green where she was to be crowned.

'Too proud, too full of her own importance.'

'Wouldn't like a son of mine to marry her.'

'Nor mine. She needs someone who'll knock it out of her.'

'I shouldn't imagine that to be possible. She'll grind her husband under her thumb right from the start.'

'Just think, some poor boy is enjoying his life – all unsuspecting.'

Six years later Liz was even more haughty and cold. Men had pursued her – rich business men as well as their sons; a film star, a racehorse owner – but they all in time became wary. Her strength of character was formidable and her suitors invariably took fright on learning more about her.

Liz did not care one jot. Men were moody, even the best of them; they were selfish, conceited and invariably unfaithful. Besides, freedom was her very life blood and the restrictions imposed by marriage were regarded by Liz with something akin to horror. No, let the Graces of this world marry and keep the race in existence. They were endowed with the procreative instinct. Liz preferred to guard her looks, protect her figure and above all, to retain her freedom.

'I'll take five.' A silver coin was tossed carelessly on to the bench serving as a counter. 'It's a raffle, I presume?'

'Your presumption's correct, sir.' Grace gave him an arch look as she handed over the tickets. 'Your chances are one in a hundred.'

A flicker of his dark eyes and then, softly,

'You'll have to explain your mathematics.'

'For every hundred tickets sold Liz here is willing to

7

give one kiss. So if we sell five hundred tickets five only will be drawn out of the bag.'

'I see.' A small pause before he said with a hint of contempt in his deep rich voice, 'I still affirm your kisses are cheap in this part of the world.'

'It's for a good cause.' Liz spoke for the first time, her voice terse, her small pointed chin high in the air. 'We've organized this Summer Fair in order to help one of the local farmers who had an accident with his tractor. He'll never farm again.'

'Accept my apologies,' he said, but in a sardonic tone which seemed to detract from the sincerity of his words. And he strode away with the easy grace of a panther, making for the exit gate leading to the field where the cars were parked.

'What an insufferable man!' Grace held the coin as if it were hot before dropping it into the box. 'I hope he isn't one of the lucky ones.'

'If his number's drawn out you can put it back.'

'As you like – wouldn't be honest, though.'

'I'm not kissing *that*!'

' "That" is supposed to kiss you,' Grace laughingly reminded her. And then she added, 'It was sporting of you to agree to this raffle, Liz. It's not in your line at all, is it?'

'Definitely not, but as Mr Carter said, it made a change from the fruit stalls and guessing the weight of a piglet – and there was no outlay.' Her expressive grey eyes followed the tall dark stranger until he disappeared from the field. She had the odd impression that he had come especially to meet her – which was ridiculous, of course. And yet she felt she had seen him before.

The sitting-room of Carlington Hall was overhung with gloom. Aunt Rose sat huddled in a chair by the great

Adam fireplace; Uncle Oliver, having in the last half-hour added at least a decade to his seventy years, kept his colourless gaze fixed on his younger niece, whose fair head was bent in an attitude of contrition and guilt. Great-Gran knitted on stolidly. At ninety-one years of age it didn't really matter if the future did look black. There couldn't be much of it to use up, anyway.

Liz only was active, her hard eyes like flint and her whole manner one of aggressive domination.

'Say something, Vivien! Don't sit there with your stupid head drooping!'

'I've s-said it all,' wailed her sister, raising a blotched and tear-stained face. 'I'm going to m-marry for love – and neither you nor anyone else is going to stop me.'

'You've always done what Liz has told you,' said Aunt Rose fretfully. 'You're fully aware that she knows what's best for you.'

'What's best for her, you mean! – what's best for all of you! I won't be used—' Vivien broke off, cowering under her sister's dark and threatening gaze. 'I'm marrying Philip,' she managed to add at length, though weakly. 'We're in love, I keep telling you that—'

'Love!' scoffed Liz. 'You've been going to the films, or watching these sloppy plays on television. Love! For heaven's sake, who wants to marry for love!'

'I do,' wailed Vivien, bursting into renewed weeping.

'I'll shake you in a minute!' Liz's mouth tightened; she took a step forward as if intending to carry out her threat, and Vivien shrank back in her chair.

'Don't bully the child,' rasped Great-Gran, squinting at her work in an endeavour to discover the reason for the hole which had suddenly appeared in her knitting. 'It's clear she intends embarking on this rash course, and after all she is old enough to please herself.'

9

'Old enough, but not sensible enough!' Liz did then move very close to her sister, and stood menacingly over her.

'You'll marry Arthur Robinson, understand?' So low her voice, like the guttural whisper of a tiger ready to spring.

Quiet sobs gave way to a wild shriek that rent the air. 'I won't – you can't make me. I love Phil—'

An exasperated sigh from Liz cut her short; Liz went over to the window and opened it, as if she required air ... or cooling off.

Water-lilies floated on the lake, which was set in a wide area of lawn. There were Japanese gardens with pagodas and flower-strewn rustic bridges, banks and banks of dazzling azaleas, almost over now but still pretty, with their light green leaves fresh and shining. There were wild gardens and herbaceous borders and avenues of trees. Some of the grounds were overgrown owing to the lack of peasant labour which had been available at the time the great hall was built in the early part of the sixteenth century.

'I'm not losing my home because of a damned silly whim of yours.' Liz turned, but Vivien was still sobbing quietly, a dripping wisp of lace held pathetically to her eyes.

'Someone should whip her,' declared Aunt Rose. 'That's what would have happened in my day.'

'Money's not all that important,' began Vivien, but was instantly silenced.

'It's the only important thing in life—'

'According to you,' Vivien wildly interrupted. 'Because you've never been in love.'

'And, thank God, I never shall be – not if this is what it does to you.'

'It's a b-beautiful feeling—'

'Spare me the details; I'm not in the least interested.'

'I don't know how you can let all this go.' Uncle Oliver spoke at last, turning a lined and hollow face in his niece's direction. 'And the money, too, just for love . . .' He shook his bald head. 'Now if you'd had the experiences I've had—'

'And you can also spare me the details,' began Liz when she herself was interrupted.

'Oliver was speaking to Vivien, not to you.' From under tired heavy lids Great-Gran peered through the distance, and Liz waited with an air of boredom for the old woman to continue. 'He likes to talk about his love affairs.'

'Love didn't do him a great deal of good,' was the sarcastic retort from Liz. 'Four wives!'

'Ah, but each one was young and fresh . . .' Uncle Oliver trailed off, his eyes glistening reflectively. 'Pity they were all after my money. I'd have been so rich today that this loss wouldn't have affected me.'

With a gesture of disgust Liz turned her back on him.

'Have you spoken to Arthur about this change of heart you're supposed to be having?' she inquired of Vivien.

'Not yet.'

'Wise girl.' Liz moved close again, to stand over the abject figure in the chair. 'Because if you had I'd have shaken the daylights out of you!'

'Someone,' said a soft voice from the open doorway, 'might at some time or other decide to shake the daylights out of you.'

Every head turned. Framed in the massive carved oak doorway stood the man at the fair.

That was how Liz described him to herself, and now a

hint of colour fused her cheeks as she recalled that kiss. A crowd had been around when the tickets were drawn, so there was no opportunity of putting that particular one back, especially as the man himself was one of the on-lookers at the draw. It should never have been put in, said Liz afterwards, but Grace asserted the unfairness of that as, previously, she had asserted the unfairness of returning the ticket to the bag.

'Not in full view of the public,' the man had declared after the two other lucky ones had given their particular brands of kisses. 'That tent over there – is it occupied?'

Her eyes had darkened.

'You'll kiss me here or not at all,' she had informed him in low and icy tones, and an odd sort of laugh had fallen from his lips.

'You'll regret it if you insist,' he warned softly, and a hush fell on the crowd standing about. What did he mean? Liz met his gaze squarely; his eyes warned even as his voice had done and for some reason Liz turned, directing her steps towards the tent which had just been vacated by the 'gipsy' fortune-teller, Mrs. Jones, who'd had to hurry back to the rectory to prepare her husband's tea.

Once inside the tent Liz faced him, her attitude one of resignation tinged with boredom. Had she voiced her thoughts the tall stranger would have heard,

'Well, what are you waiting for? Get it over and done with, for heaven's sake!'

She did not voice her thoughts, and yet he might have read them, for he proceeded with maddening slowness to take her in his arms. And even then he held her for a while, looking searchingly into her eyes. Presently his lips were on her mouth, moderately gentle at first, but as she stiffened he seemed to become possessed of an ardour – or perhaps it was anger at being treated in this insolent way. Whatever the driving force his kiss became brutal and demanding and Liz began to struggle in his arms. They were hawsers of steel, and strong as she was she could not free herself. Fury raged within her; she would have struck him if she could, but her arms were locked to her sides, crushed against her slender body.

'Hmm ...' A half-sneer of amusement touched the outline of his mouth. 'Not bad – for a penny. I shall remember your bargain offer, Miss – er—?'

It was only afterwards that Liz suddenly gained the impression that he did in fact know her name. For the present she lifted her head haughtily, and the arrogant sweep of her eyes should by rights have reduced him to a corpse. She then left the tent, her body aflame with the rage that seethed at his outrageous treatment of her.

And now here he was – in the house.

'What the devil are you doing here?' she frowningly inquired on recovering from her astonishment.

'The front door was open. I did think of ringing but felt the bell would not be heard above the noise going on in the house.' He advanced further into the room, apparently oblivious of the stares of the people about him. His eyes wandered all around, taking in the furnishings, and the situation, in the one, all-embracing glance. Massive antique furniture and rare paintings on the wall; wainscoting and the impression of secret panels; silver and china and all else that spelled great wealth. Then the huddled girl, sobbing in the chair; the wizened hunchback grasping the knitting-needles in its claws; the disgruntled man and doleful woman . . . and Liz. 'The name's Nigel Shapani—'

'Nigel!' gasped Vivien. 'From Greece – Arthur's brother?'

'Half-brother,' he snapped, as if even that relationship were repugnant to him.

Liz looked at him intently. So that was why she had thought she'd seen him before! There was a faint resemblance to his half-brother, although Arthur was all English whereas Nigel's father was obviously Greek.

'You never told us Arthur had a brother.' Liz turned accusingly to her sister, who was drying her eyes and peeping up at Nigel now and then as if searching for some sign that she had an ally.

'You were never interested—'

'I was always interested in anything to do with Arthur, naturally, seeing that you were engaged to him. Why didn't you mention this – this—?' She broke off as Nigel's dark brows shot up. 'Why didn't you say he had a brother?' she asked, throwing Nigel a glance as arrogant as his own.

'I didn't know about him myself at first. Then by the time Arthur did mention him I knew I wanted to break the engagement, so there was no point in telling you of him.' She stopped speaking rather abruptly because of the look Liz directed at her. However, she was left in peace for a while as Liz gave her attention to the man who had so unceremoniously entered the house.

'Why are you here? Am I to understand you've flown over from Greece in order to sort this matter out?'

'My brother informed me of a quarrel having taken place between him and Vivien here – and although she hadn't said so outright, he gained the impression that she no longer wanted to marry him.' Nigel's glance strayed to Vivien. 'I appear to have arrived at an inopportune moment. I desire to take this matter up with someone in private.'

'On the contrary, you've come at a most opportune

14

moment,' commented Liz in terse emphatic tones. 'You can discuss the matter with Vivien – in public.'

He threw her a sidelong glance, it stripped her insolently and her nostrils quivered.

'In public, eh?' He looked around. 'What have we here—?' A careless gesture of his hand embraced the other silent three. 'A deaf and dumb school?'

Liz gritted her teeth.

'They're not concerned in this.'

'They all stand to lose their home – and a nice fat legacy.'

'Don't!' shrieked Aunt Rose, jerking up in her chair and then flopping back again. 'Poverty at my age – Oh, woe is me – woe is me!'

Nigel looked at her as if she were slightly deranged, as well he might, seeing as she was now rocking to and fro, still muttering those last words despairingly to herself.

'Nigel,' whispered Vivien entreatingly, 'are you on my side?' So pathetic she looked, and frail, and a smile actually appeared to soften the harshness of that thin half-sneering mouth. He ignored her question though, and said,

'You're in love with someone else—? Yes, I stood in the hall a moment or two, so I did gather that you now desire to marry for love.'

'She is marrying,' interposed Liz softly, 'for money.'

Nigel frowned darkly at her.

'Do you mind keeping out of this?' he snapped authoritatively, and Liz's eyes flashed fire. But she was extremely puzzled by the man's unconcern, and she said, watching him intently,

'You also stand to lose a fortune if our families are not united by marriage. Don't you care about losing all your money?'

'As I don't keep all my eggs in one basket I shan't be losing all my money.' He paused a moment, and a sudden frown became fixed upon his brow. 'Nevertheless, I stand to lose a considerable sum, an eventuality which impelled me to come over and see what could be done. Vivien, couldn't you possibly marry Arthur? I must own that I do understand your aversion, but if you don't marry him you yourself will lose your share, which I'm sure you know is almost as considerable as my own.'

'I don't care about the money. I want to marry for love.' Tears stood on her lashes again and Nigel's eyes softened momentarily.

'Have you ever heard of such nonsense?' demanded Aunt Rose of no one in particular. 'Marrying for love!'

'It does seem a rather antiquated idea,' agreed Nigel with a yawn. 'Must you marry for love, child?'

'I've said so – many times.' She looked up at him from under fluttering lashes. 'I'm sorry . . . very sorry . . .'

Liz uttered an exasperated sigh. For the first time in her life she was beaten, and in her fury and frustration she directed her invective against those who were dead.

'Idiots, both of them! Love and goodwill; forgiveness and the burying of antagonism, as that stupid great-grandfather of mine termed it—'

'Now, Liz, none of that! My husband was a devout and pious man. He made that will with the best of intentions.'

Liz had not the patience to comment and a silence fell on the room. Her great-grandfather and Nigel's great-grandfather on his mother's side had quarrelled when at school, and for over forty years had not spoken to one another. Then Liz's great-grandfather had been persuaded to join the Pious Fellowship of Friends whose slogan was, 'Forgiveness is your sure passport to heaven,' and as old

Archibald had lived a far from blameless life he naturally suffered deep concern regarding his passport to heaven. And so he became a member, only to find that his old enemy was also desirous of journeying safely to heaven. The consequence was that the hatchet was buried and for the last few years of their lives the two men were staunch friends. But during those previous years the younger members of both families had formed their own barriers. Not that it mattered, for they rarely came into contact with one another. However, to the two recruits to the Fellowship this state of affairs seemed altogether wrong. Moreover, should they be blamed by the High Council for the animosity existing between the two families, they might not have their passports stamped after all.

There was only one thing to be done, declared the administrator of the Fellowship on being consulted by the two. They must bring about a reconciliation between their families, and the simplest way was for them to be united by marriage.

Consternation broke out when on the death of Archibald the will was read, but of course things remained as they were until the death of Septimus a year later.

'You'll have to marry Arthur,' Liz had instantly declared, and with her customary submissiveness towards the stronger sister who, although only two years her senior, had always been able to dominate her, Vivien offered no resistance. Arthur too, was agreeable, having no wish to lose a vast fortune by acting contrary to his great-grandfather's wishes.

The marriage was arranged and about to go through without a hitch when, to the amazement of all concerned, Vivien came in one day saying she had met someone else and intended marrying him.

'Both families will be bankrupt!' said Liz unbelievingly. 'All our money going to the Fellowship! No, my girl, you'll do as you're told and marry Arthur.'

As far as Liz was concerned that ended the matter, but Vivien and Phil met in secret, Vivien not having sufficient courage to break the engagement, so great was her fear of Liz. But at last the secret could be kept no longer, for the wedding must take place within the next five weeks. And so the showdown occurred, with Liz pacing the floor like a raging lion, repeating her warnings and threats which, to her great chagrin, resulted merely in reducing Vivien to tears but certainly not to submission.

'You've just said you didn't mention your change of heart to Arthur.' Liz turned to Vivien at last, eyeing her curiously.

'That's true, I didn't, but we did quarrel, and he's acted strangely once or twice recently, as if sensing that there was something wrong.' Vivien tilted her face to look up at Nigel. 'He must have guessed – and sent for you?'

'That's right, he did guess you wished to break the engagement. I flew over this morning and Arthur informed me you'd both be at the village fair, so I had my lunch with him and then went on to this fair.' He turned his face to Liz as he spoke and she found to her annoyance that she could not suppress the flush which rose to her cheeks at the mockery she saw there. In turn, her blush brought a sardonic twist to his lips and her small fists clenched. Liz would dearly have loved to strike him a vicious and wounding blow. 'After inquiring around I eventually discovered your sister,' he went on to inform Vivien. 'But I couldn't find you.'

'I was in the marquee, judging the Bonny Babies.'

His lips quivered, but he said gravely, 'An entertainment I missed. How very disappointing.'

Liz looked sharply at him, but his face was now expressionless. Had he a sense of humour? she wondered, noticing that Vivien was also looking at him, uncertainty in her eyes.

'I think you're laughing at me,' she murmured, lowering her head to hide her embarrassment.

'Indeed, no,' he denied in the same grave tones. 'I'm only sorry I missed this – er – Bonny Baby competition—'

'Can we forget the Bonny Babies and return to the important matter of Vivien's marriage?' intervened Uncle Oliver testily. 'This is no time for frivolities, sir! Are we all to be reduced to penury, or is it in your power to do something with that obstinate, selfish girl?'

'No one can do anything with me!' flashed Vivien, seeming to have taken courage all at once from Nigel's presence. 'I don't care about my personal losses, and as for you – you'll all have to go into an old folks' home—'

'A home?' cried Aunt Rose. 'Oh, no – no – *no*!'

'Rose, stop that screaming,' rasped Great-Gran. 'I've dropped a stitch and I'll never be able to pick it up. Liz, do it for me!'

Liz's teeth snapped together, but she went over to the old woman and took the knitting from her. It was several minutes before she managed to rectify Great-Gran's mistake.

'There you are. Now be more careful . . .' Liz tailed off, aware of Nigel's gaze upon her. Straightening up, she looked directly at him . . . and wondered at the odd expression she encountered in those dark and steely eyes.

'Mr. Shapani,' Aunt Rose was saying, 'do something with Vivien! Do something, *please* – for if I go into a home I shall die within a week!'

Nigel's gaze was still fixed upon Liz; she sat down, continuing to hold that gaze for some moments, but then she had to look away, twisting one shoe daintily and regarding it as if she had discovered something exceedingly interesting about it.

'The child wants to marry for love,' said Nigel at last, a strange note in his voice. 'There's nothing anyone can do about it.'

Vivien stared unbelievingly at him, her blue eyes bright and clear as a star.

'You're on my side,' she breathed wonderingly. 'I'm so very glad you decided to come.'

'But what can we do?' whined Uncle Oliver. 'As Rose said, she couldn't live in a home, and neither could I.'

Liz glared at Nigel, who merely smiled to himself . . . a smile of satisfaction which puzzled her immensely.

'It won't come to that,' she declared emphatically. 'We must think of something to beat those two half-witted old fools!'

Nigel's eyes were again fixed upon her.

'Has it ever occurred to you that you could go out and work for a living?' he inquired mildly.

'This vast fortune can't go to that idiotic Fellowship,' she snapped, ignoring his question.

'I agree it's an appalling waste,' Nigel looked round the room at the various members of the family in turn. 'There are others who could serve our purpose—' His eyes came to rest on Aunt Rose and Liz frowned at his expression. She was not left long in this state of perplexity. 'I've an uncle somewhere who might consider marriage. He's not a beneficiary, but he might oblige for a small remuneration. Madam, could you bring yourself to marry again?'

'Again?' She glared at him and her round little virgin body became upright in the chair. 'I've never been married, young man, and I've more sense than to enter into that unpredictable state at sixty-eight years of age.'

'You have?' Nigel's amused glance flickered to Uncle Oliver. 'What about you? I've an aunt—'

'Then you can keep her,' the old man interrupted. 'Four, I've had – and that last one was enough to put me off for the rest of my life. No, young feller,' he ended emphatically, 'you can count me out.'

Watching Nigel's face with interest, Liz wondered what he was about. Something strange here, she concluded, and for apparently no reason at all her spine began to tingle.

'Grandma?' he queried slowly, turning away from Liz. Her eyes glinted. She was sure his face portrayed suppressed laughter. 'You—?'

'It's Great-Gran,' submitted Vivien obligingly, and Nigel made a swift apology.

'Sorry. Great-Gran, then. How's she fixed?'

Liz pursed her lips. Nigel still avoided her gaze and she would have given anything to read his face.

'She's ninety-one!' gasped Vivien.

'Ninety-one? Really?' He shrugged his shoulders in a gesture of resignation. 'Well, I suppose she is a bit past it.' He transferred his attention to Vivien, then he looked straight at her sister, the most odd expression in his eyes.

'What did you say?' Great-Gran peered at Nigel. 'Vivien, tell me what's going on! I've been concentrating on my work – and in any case my hearing's not as good as it was. What did he say? Answer me at once!'

'He said you're past it,' obliged Vivien unthinkingly.

'What?' A frail hand bent the lobe of a purple-veined ear into a forward position. 'Speak up, girl, speak up!'

'He says you're past it!' shouted Uncle Oliver.

'Past it?' The old woman glared interrogatingly at Nigel. 'Past what?'

'Cut out the tomfoolery,' snapped Liz. 'This is no time for making jokes.'

The room became silent except for the low disgusted sniffs issuing from Aunt Rose now and then as she went over Nigel's suggestion that she should marry his uncle. Nigel moved after a while, taking possession of one end of the couch. Liz was sitting at the other end and there was a wide space between them. But she glanced sideways at him, and in the glow from a setting sun his face took on an almost satanic aspect; she thought of that kiss – and shuddered. He turned an expressionless face towards her.

'There appears to be only one other solution to the problem,' he remarked calmly, at last.

Uncle Oliver and Aunt Rose leant forward in their chairs expectantly.

'You've thought of something?' inquired the old man on an eager note.

Liz's eyes widened in disbelief even as Nigel's mouth twitched with amusement.

'I have,' he returned in that lazy, drawling tone, 'but I rather think my idea has no appeal for the young lady concerned.'

'Perhaps,' challenged Liz after a pause, 'you'll be a little more explicit?'

Nigel flicked a speck of dust from his sleeve.

'The idea is,' he murmured, faintly bored, 'for you and me to marry.'

Great-Gran's knitting needles clicked; they sounded like the cracking of whips, so profound was the silence which dropped after Nigel's calm statement had been voiced.

Vivien was the first to speak, the electrified atmosphere plainly being lost on her.

'Liz won't ever get married. She's not the marrying kind.'

'Often said she wouldn't be burdened with the restrictions marriage imposes,' supplemented Uncle Oliver. 'Besides, she doesn't like men – thinks they're selfish and shallow and too imbued with the idea of their own importance.'

'Confirmed spinster.' Aunt Rose shook her head sadly. 'I thought you'd found a way out of our difficulties, but it's no use considering Liz as an answer.'

'What's going on, eh?' Great-Gran peered over her spectacles. 'Speak up, I won't be left out of the conversation like this. Liz, what are you saying?'

'I haven't spoken a word for several minutes,' she said between her teeth.

'Nigel wants to marry her.' Vivien leant right over and spoke into the old woman's ear.

'Nigel? Who's he?'

'This young man.' Aunt Rose pointed to him. 'If he and Liz married our problems would be solved, but Liz won't marry anybody.'

'What's wrong with this Nigel?' Great-Gran peered harder. 'Looks all right to me. Take him, Liz, and let's have no more fuss about this matter.'

'Don't be ridiculous!' With a distasteful glance at Nigel Liz moved from the couch to the window and stood looking out. To lose everything – this home and a vast fortune ... No one in their right mind would throw it all away. And there were the old people, especially Great-Gran, with whom she had always been close. Liz had a reputation for being hard, but old age had always touched some chord within her – dragging at it so that it hurt abominably. Turning her head, she looked at Great-Gran.

The old lady's hearing and eyesight were failing and her heart had given her trouble lately. Only one or two years left at most. She could not spend them in a home. Nor could she be left all day – should Liz contemplate going out to work and having Great-Gran with her. Liz glanced at her aunt and uncle in turn; she was not quite so perturbed about them, but Great-Gran . . . Liz shook her head. There really was only an institution . . . unless . . .

Transferring her gaze to Nigel, Liz saw that he watched her intently and knew he had guessed at the struggle taking place within her.

'We could marry,' she murmured reluctantly at last, 'and live apart.'

The others threw her astounded looks – all except Great-Gran, who had not heard.

'We could,' agreed Nigel at length, then slowly shook his head. 'But I am not willing to enter into that sort of contract.'

She frowned, recalling his hateful kiss. The contemplation of anything more was revolting.

'In that case,' she said through tight lips, 'we must all face up to the loss of our fortunes.'

Silence, with hope once again dying on the faces of the others. Vivien gazed soulfully at her hands. She was free to marry the man of her choice and she considered all well lost for love.

'Perhaps,' suggested Nigel, rising from the couch, 'we could discuss this matter more comfortably in private.'

'There's nothing to discuss. I'd never consider living with you as your wife.' Dark and formidable he looked, like some pagan god resurrected from the mists of Greek history.

His mouth compressed at the disdain in her voice. Nevertheless, he repeated his question for a private discussion and with a shrug of resignation Liz led the way into a small study that had once been her father's, and which only she herself now used.

'Take a seat,' she invited stiffly.

He pulled out a chair for her and they both sat down opposite to one another.

'I said I wouldn't agree to the sort of marriage you suggested,' he then began without preamble. 'But I didn't say I wanted you as my wife in every sense of the word.' He paused a moment to let that sink in before continuing, 'One cannot possibly marry and immediately separate – there are one's friends to think of, if nothing else. They would consider it very odd indeed, I'm sure you'll agree with me about that?'

'My friends would know the reason for the marriage, so there'd be no question of their considering it odd that my husband was not with me.' Her lovely face was pale, her hands were clenched tightly in her lap.

'Unfortunately I am not in a similar position.' He hesitated and Liz gained the impression that he could very well have fallen in with her suggestion but did not want to do so. 'If I marry I must take my wife back to Greece with me.'

'For appearance? But need you tell your friends you're married?'

He glanced away, avoiding the intense scrutiny with which she regarded him.

'I cannot see myself living a lie for the rest of my life. No, my dear, if we marry then you must accompany me back to Greece.'

Liz spread her hands. She did not mention her concern for the old ones as she said, disgusted at the uncontrollable

25

tremor in her voice. 'What will I gain? It's my home I want. I love it – and the money? – I want to spend it and enjoy life. No—' She shook her head emphatically. 'I won't marry you unless we can part immediately after the wedding.'

'You'll allow two fortunes to pass into the hands of strangers?' he asked softly and, when she did not answer, 'You say you love your home and that's what you want. But if you don't marry me you'll lose it anyway. If you do marry me at least it will be there and you can visit it periodically. I understand the house itself comes to you when anything happens to your relatives?'

'Yes, it's part of my share. Great-Grandfather knew how much I loved it.'

'Well then, think before making your decision. Do you really want to see this house sold to strangers, and the money go to the Fellowship?'

At the mention of the Fellowship her fury rose. If only her great-grandfather had not become mixed up with those lunatics!

'It seems to me,' she said after a long and thoughtful silence, 'that whatever I do I'm going to be the loser.'

'Thanks,' he returned sardonically, and leant back in his chair.

'You know very well I don't want to marry you,' she retorted, 'so the exception you take to my words is misplaced.'

'We had better keep the discussion amicable,' he recommended, 'otherwise we're not going to get very far.'

She looked oddly at him.

'You sound as if you *want* to marry me,' she said at length.

'Then I must inadvertently have misled you,' was the smooth rejoinder, and a flush leapt to her cheeks. 'I've no more desire to acquire a wife than you have to acquire a husband, but like you, I hate the thought of all that money slipping through my fingers.' He paused a moment and she again experienced that tingle in the region of her spine. He had at first stated emphatically that he did not have all his eggs in one basket, and in fact he appeared unperturbed about his own personal loss. Yet now he was really trying to sway her, to persuade her into marriage because – so he said – he hated the idea of all that money slipping through his fingers. Could he have some other motive for wanting her to marry him? she wondered, suddenly wary. He was half Greek, and the Greeks were notoriously the most amorous race in the world . . . That kiss . . . desire there, primitive and savage desire . . . But she could stick up for herself. He could not force her into something without her co-operation – or could he? That embrace was surely proof enough that his strength was not to be scorned. 'Neither of us would trouble the other,' he said, breaking into her thoughts as if he were actually reading them. 'We'll live in the same house, and be amicable when my friends are around, but otherwise we shall go our separate ways.' He stopped, waiting for some comment, but did not meet her gaze. She was still puzzled by something she could not name. He appeared genuine enough, and yet . . . 'It seems a reasonable course to take,' he was saying. 'The only course, if we're not to lose both of these fortunes.' He did look at her now, straight in the eye, and Liz was reassured. He had no more desire for her than she had for him, and as he said, this was the reasonable course to take.

'I always swore I'd never give up my freedom,' she said with a deep sigh.

He laughed softly, and she stared at him in wonderment. What a transformation in his features!

27

'Strangely, so did I. But there you are – the best laid plans . . . None of us can foresee the future and the problems it casts in our way.' He paused. 'Are we engaged?' he inquired with a humorous lift of his brows.

Liz refused to give him an immediate answer; she must consider the matter carefully, she said.

But as she gazed up into those green eyes she had the disquieting conviction that this dark pagan from the wild country of Parnassus was going to play a major role in shaping her destiny.

CHAPTER TWO

THEY had left Athens behind, travelling along a road bordering that incredible 'wine-dark' sea of Greece, while in the hazy distance rose the small mass of polychromic splendour that was the island of Aegina, and, closer to, the island of Salamis.

'You've been to Greece before?' Nigel spoke with that lazy drawl which had already begun to grate on his wife's nerves, for it seemed to emphasize the indifference with which he intended to regard her.

'I had a holiday in Athens once.' Her tone was cold and uninviting and a long silence fell between them again, with Nigel concentrating on his driving and Liz dwelling with a sort of savage frustration on her great-grandfather and the cranks with whom he had latterly associated.

All her life she had to stay with this man by her side! Her freedom curtailed – and through no fault of her own!

She tried to calm the fury within her, telling herself that the monotony would be periodically relieved by her visits to her home in England. A sideways glance at her husband's carved profile made her think again. She would be bored . . . Oh, so immeasurably bored with this creature always around! Her hands were clenched in her lap; she was not aware of this until Nigel said, as they were taking a sharp, magnificent climb on the road which would eventually bring them into the Parnassus country,

'What the devil's wrong with you? Relax, for the lord's sake. I'm not used to riding with a block of ice beside me.' Still the slow lazy drawl, and the hint of an accent to emphasize it.

Liz glared at the dark profile and flashed,

'There was nothing in our contract that said I must entertain you!'

'Entertain?' A sideways flick of the dark head revealed the amusement in his grey-green eyes. 'Shouldn't think you could be very entertaining . . . in any way.'

Her eyes opened wide, anger rising again. But she coloured too, because of the subtle insinuation he had made.

'I'm glad you realize it,' she snapped, and looked out of the window. They were descending now, passing through the incredible scenery that only Greece can display. Valleys alternated with hills on which the exquisite greys and greens of olives and cypresses, vines and poplars blended to form a breathtakingly beautiful panorama of subdued colour which made a splendid backcloth for the walled *castro* standing out against the flawless sapphire of a Grecian sky.

'I hope,' said Nigel, changing gear rapidly as he took a hairpin bend, 'that you're not expecting a situation where we'll remain coldly isolated from one another for the rest of our lives?'

She twisted sharply, her nerves becoming taut.

'You gave me to understand that would be the position.'

Nigel changed up again, remaining in third gear before having to negotiate another acute bend a few hundreds yards further along the road.

'On the contrary, I believe I mentioned we'd be amicable when my friends were around.' Something in the way he said that brought a sudden frown to her eyes. And yet what had she to fear? She was strong-willed, and in physique she was not exactly puny, her slenderness and delicate feminine curves being deceptive, for Liz had developed muscle by swimming, playing tennis and climbing.

Nigel was obviously awaiting some comment and she said, still in that icy tone which was now deliberately edged with hostility,

'As long as you don't expect me to be too amicable you won't be disappointed.' She saw his mouth compress, felt the car jerk forward as his foot went down on the accelerator.

'I hope, Liz,' he said in a very soft tone, 'that we shall manage to understand one another from the start. I'm neither a patient man nor an easy-going one; on the contrary, I've a reputation for obduracy and so perhaps a timely warning would save us both a good deal of unpleasantness.'

She bristled. The pomposity of the man! Anyone would think he was *really* her husband! The urge to lash out with her tongue and put him in his place once and for all was strong, but she curbed it, saying instead, with quiet sarcasm,

'I'm afraid I must be extraordinarily obtuse, for I fail to grasp your meaning.'

The ghost of a smile touched the stern outline of his mouth.

'You fail to get the message,' he corrected softly.

'What's the difference?'

'There is a subtle one, Liz – and it behoves you to take care.'

She turned, her blue eyes flashing and a little hiss of anger escaping from between clenched teeth.

'Don't threaten me! I've no idea what you're trying to convey, but you'll be wise to leave me alone. You said we should go our separate ways, and that's exactly what I intend doing. I've never had any desire to be married – men bore me to distraction with their inane conversation – if you could describe the one-sided egotistical prating as conversation. The years spent with you must be endured through the stupidity of a man!' she went on furiously. '*Endured,* get that – for I shall find every single moment unbearable!'

Silence, with an atmosphere that could be cut with a knife. And then,

'Let us hope that some moments won't prove to be more unbearable than others,' he murmured, pulling right over as a car approached from the opposite direction.

'And what,' she demanded in low vibrating tones, 'do you mean by that?' No answer, just an exasperated sigh as if the conversation had suddenly become irritating to him. He appeared absorbed in the scenery – the green-clothed foothills and higher naked peaks, the wide cultivated plains and deep ravines, with the stream in the distance, sparkling in the sunshine like a twisted silver ribbon.

'So you've never had any desire to be married...' When at last Nigel spoke it was in the familiar softly-drawling tone but so low now that Liz scarcely caught the words. 'Not normal—' she did catch that and swiftly interrupted him.

'I'm quite normal! But I suppose you, as a Greek – or half Greek,' she amended as he shot her a glance, 'I suppose you consider a woman's lot to be nothing more nor less than that of a chattel. She was born to satisfy some man's desire, to bear him numerous children and to remain always subservient to his wishes. Well, that might be your idea, but it doesn't serve in the West. Women now have their own lives and they live them as they choose. It so happens that I choose to remain a spinster!'

'A spinster?' he repeated, his voice edged with laughter. 'You appear to have forgotten something.'

Crimson colour flooded her face. She *had* forgotten — for a few brief seconds.

'I still consider myself a spinster,' she flashed, aware of the childishness of that, and his amused laugh was expected – though angrily resented.

'You're very much married, Liz.' No more was said for a long while as they travelled the narrow road, taking bend after bend, with the landscape becoming more solitary and more spectacular with every mile covered. It was a vast primitive world of departed gods – gods like the handsome Dionysos, whose grandfather, Cadmus, had founded the citadel of Thebes. Dionysos himself had been rescued from his dying mother's womb and sewn into the thigh of his father, the mighty Zeus, king of all the gods of Olympus.

His cult was one of orgiastic rites; he represented all that was irrational in man in contrast to his unsullied half-brother, Apollo, who stood for all that was honourable and dignified in the human race. It was a vast unreal world, a world where one found isolation at its most sublime, a world of colour contrasts, of wild spectacular heights, alternating with valleys and wide ochre-flooded plains.

They travelled on and now there would appear a shepherd on a lonely hillside, guiding his sheep and goats with his long crooked stick. And then an isolated *khani* appeared as they took another bend in the road and Nigel slowed the car down to a crawl as he approached it.

'Do you want something to drink?'

'No, thank you.' She was being deliberately obstinate, knowing full well that Nigel wanted a drink. He could go without, she decided, and sat back in her seat. 'It'll waste time. I'd rather carry on; the sun's already going down.'

Nigel drew to the side of the road and tucked the car right in.

'We have all the time in the world,' he commented, sliding one long leg from the car. He stood up and closed the car door and said, without much expression, 'Excuse me, won't you? Unlike you, I'm ready for some refreshment.' And he left her sitting there, fuming with rage that her first attempt at demonstrating her will had failed.

A few minutes later she had to watch him comfortably seated outside the *cafeneion,* under the shade of a huge plane tree, drinking from a tall glass and conversing with another customer sitting at the next table. Her throat felt parched and she was swallowing when Nigel looked across, amusement on his face. He was no fool. He knew she was dying with thirst! Her fists clenched. If the look she threw at him had proved effective he'd instantly have slumped forward in his chair!

Nigel did not hurry himself and it was half an hour before they were on their way again, Liz seething inwardly and with a shrewd suspicion that Nigel was fully aware of this.

'We haven't too far to go now,' he said as they reached Levadia. 'Only about thirty miles. I expect you're tired?'

She chose not to reply and once more they drove in silence, but in spite of herself Liz could not but be enthralled by the scenic beauty of the landscape. Ahead loomed the mighty Parnassus, that 'compassionate' mountain that had gathered in the fallen Sanctuary of Delphi when, by the edict of Theodosios the Great, the heathen cult was prohibited. The mountain summits glistened, for snow still veiled the highest points. After proceeding through a narrow pass they emerged into a widening valley and then climbed towards the watershed. After crossing the spur of Parnassus a gorge unfolded before them and the town of Arachova came colourfully into view, clinging to the mountain over three thousand feet above sea level. It was the 'Windy Town' of the ancient Greeks, the town of which was written, 'They are all shepherds and shepherdesses, who feed their sheep upon the mountains.'

'This is a pretty town, don't you think?' said Nigel conversationally as they drove through it. Liz glanced at him, wondering if he were bored with the long silence or if he genuinely wished to make the journey more pleasant for her. Liz's first reaction was to ignore his comment, but on second thoughts she decided there was no sense in deliberately creating antagonism between them. Their feelings for one another on entering this mercenary contract had been those of complete indifference, and this was the way they must endeavour to continue. Civility was desirable, for life would probably prove difficult enough anyway, without the added intrusion of hostility that must inevitably lead to frayed tempers and heated arguments.

'It is pretty,' she agreed as they entered the main street. It splashed colour with its rugs – for which the town was famous – and with its embroidery and Greek urns and the whole assortment of tourist goods. 'I like the cobbled streets and the little streams.' On all levels the terraces blazed with colour, many of the flowers being grown in petrol cans or other tin containers.

After that they chatted in a more friendly fashion until they reached Kastri, built when the excavations of the sacred shrine of Apollo necessitated the removal of the village of Delphi, what at that time stood on the actual site of the sun god's sanctuary.

Nigel's house was above the town of Kastri, a spreading one-storeyed building of weathered limestone, and planned round a pillared courtyard bright with flowers and shaded by vines. On the air hung the heady fragrance of basil mingling with the sweet scent of oleanders growing on a dry bank at the far side of the extensive grounds. Soaring above were the 'Shining Ones', the twin peaks of the mountain, pink-misted now in the strange reflected light from a lowering sun, and even as Liz stood there, her appreciative gaze fixed upon the towering heights, the pink changed to clouded pearl upon which in turn was superimposed a soft translucent mauve.

A strange peace fell upon Liz, despite the convulsed landscape and the ragged heights in which nested the birds of prey – buzzards and eagles. The courtyard was cool after the hot tiring journey, the quietness was profound, broken only by the play of the fountains and the hum of insects busy among the flowers.

'It's very lovely.' Liz turned to Nigel and looked up. How tall he was! It gave her a feeling of inferiority, having to tilt her head like this.

'You like it?' He smiled in some amusement, looking her over for a space as if seeing her properly for the first time. 'Not as palatial as your home – but when I had it renovated it was merely for myself – a bachelor establishment.'

She looked away and said,

'But you have plenty of rooms? You must have guests sometimes?'

Nigel laughed then, and clapped his hands for his servant.

'I did, naturally, have guests in mind. We're not short of bedrooms.'

At that Liz would have put aside her good resolutions

36

and paid him back with some sarcastic retort, but at that moment a manservant appeared and Nigel spoke to him.

'My wife, Nikos—'

'Your – wife, Mr. Nigel?' The man started, evincing not mere surprise but amazement to a degree that brought a frown to Liz's brow. Nigel might already have been married, so amazed and disbelieving was the man's expression.

However, he recovered and Liz received a smile as he said, in broken English,

'Pleased to meet you, Mrs. Nigel. You are welcome.'

'Thank you, Nikos.' Transferring her gaze, Liz looked at her husband. His chiselled features were impassive as, with an imperious yet careless geture, he indicated the car.

'Unload our bags, Nikos. And show my wife to the White Room.'

Another strange glance and then,

'Certainly, Mr. Nigel.'

The White Room was breathtaking. Walls and ceiling were white, also the paintwork, but the furniture was in a pastel shade of peach, as was the carpet and curtains. The bathroom off was a dream in peach and dove grey, with an enormous bath and separate shower.

'Will there be anything you want, Mrs. Nigel?'

She shook her head, wondering what he was thinking, for there was only a single bed in the room, and no connecting door into any other apartment.

'No, thank you, Nikos.'

'Shall I send my wife up to unpack your cases?'

'I'll do that myself, thank you.'

He went out, softly closing the door, and Liz moved over to the window and stepped out on to the railed balcony on which was a small table and a comfortable arm-chair. Baskets of flowers hung from brackets fixed to the corner opposite and to the wall of the house. Flowers in earthenware pots stood at the ends of the balcony, and a vine twisted its way through the wrought-iron railings. She stood looking out over the grey sea of olives sweeping across the Plain of Amphissa to the Bay of Itea, and the blue waters of the Corinthian Gulf. It was an idyllic picture, with the tremendous cliffs of Parnassus shadowed now as the sun's rays slanted low, bringing a softness to the eagle crags and the gorge, above which rose in sheer majesty the two great peaks of the Phaedriades.

Re-entering the room at last, Liz unpacked her suitcases and after taking a bath and changing into a cool cotton dress, sleeveless and short, she came out into the wide corridor and glanced uncertainly around.

'Mrs. Nigel . . .' Nikos appeared and indicated she should follow him, which she did, and they entered the dining-room where Nigel was standing against the window, one hand resting on the frame, the other thrust into his pocket. He was gazing out over the same view as was seen from Liz's bedroom, but he turned at her entry and his eyes swept from the shining mass of hair to the dainty sandals on her feet. 'Shall I serve dinner now, Mr. Nigel?'

'Please, Nikos.' The servant disappeared and Nigel asked Liz what she would like to drink.

She asked for sherry, taking possession of the chair by the window which Nigel indicated. He sat down opposite to her, his eyes thoughtful, his lips pursed. Liz felt strange, caught in an unreal situation, and she fell to thinking of the wedding, so quiet and swift, with just her own family present, all except Great-Gran who could not make the journey to the church.

The day before the wedding Liz had questioned Nigel as to his attitude towards the eventual dissolving of the marriage. He was firm and inflexible in his pronouncement that the marriage was permanent. He was more Greek than English, he said, and in his country people did not enter into marriage with the idea that it could easily be dissolved.

She thought about this. It wasn't really important. She would never require her freedom, so there was no point in starting off an argument at this late stage in the proceedings. If Nigel wished to remain tied for life, then that was all right with her.

'The dinner, Mr. Nigel.' Nikos waited until they sat down at the table and then served them, going first to Nigel, whose flick of a hand sent him, surprised, to Liz.

After dinner Nigel went out and Liz stayed on the patio reading until ten o'clock and then she went to bed. She was bored already, she realized, and wondered how on earth her future was going to be endured.

CHAPTER THREE

NIGEL had business in Athens requiring his attention and three days after her arrival in Kastri Liz was on her own. This did not trouble her; on embarking on this marriage she had neither expected nor desired the company of her husband. In this house she had imagined herself rather in the position of a guest, and could she have had her way Liz would have chosen separate apartments altogether, but the house was comparatively small, and consequently not adaptable to the conversion Liz had in mind.

Already she had made a tour of the Sanctuary, an experience she would never forget. It was true that Delphi was Greece's most magnificent site – and she felt it was no exaggeration when people declared the setting to be one of the most spectacular in the world.

Liz was sitting at her dressing-table, manicuring her nails, when Maria, Nikos's wife, knocked timidly and opened the door in response to Liz's 'come in'.

With a rather frightened expression on her face, the Greek woman said in very broken English,

'Where is Mr. Nigel? My husband is out and I look everywhere for Mr. Nigel.'

'He's also out. What is it, Maria?'

'Out? *Ah . . . alímono!*' The woman clasped her hands together. 'There is a visitor, Mrs. Nigel – and she storms, you know, because she wants to see Mr. Nigel. My husband not tell me Mr. Nigel go out. *Alímono!* What are we to do?'

'She storms?' Liz stood up, and stared at the woman. Surely nothing less than a catastrophe could produce an expression like that. Liz's eyes flickered past her; Nikos had appeared and on his face too there was the same half-scared expression.

'What does *ah, alímono* mean?' she asked, frowning. 'Maria just said it,' she explained as he threw her a questioning glance.

'It means, oh, alas!' Nikos pushed his wife out of the way. 'Mrs. Nigel, there is someone to see your husband, and although I've told her he's away from home she refuses to go. She wants to see you.'

'Who is she?' Liz was recalling Nikos's startled manner on Nigel's introducing his wife to him.

'She – she—' Nikos licked his lips. 'What shall I do?' he asked hastily, and Liz's frown deepened.

'I asked you who she is.' Liz looked straight at him, very much in the manner she had looked at Vivien when trying to force her into marriage with Nigel's brother. 'Tell me immediately, if you please.'

The man darted a glance at his wife. She moved silently away, to disappear as she made hurriedly towards the region of the kitchen.

'She's – she's— Her name's Greta, and she's Mr. Nigel's ...' The man tailed off, lowering his eyes.

'His girl-friend?' said Liz, recalling Nigel's passionate, demanding kiss. It didn't surprise her that he had a girl-friend. In fact, it would have very much surprised her if he had not.

Nikos glanced up, somewhat bewildered.

'You're not angry, Mrs. Nigel?'

She looked rather haughtily at him, having no intention of entering into this sort of conversation with a servant.

'Take the lady into the salon. Tell her I'll be with her in a few minutes.'

'Yes, Mrs. Nigel, certainly.' But at the door he turned. 'I

shall be in the kitchen – if you should want me.'

A faint smile touched her lips. Did he think she might need protection?

'Thank you, Nikos, I'll remember that.'

She dressed, brushed her hair and went out and along to the front hall, off which was the salon. The girl was standing with her back to the room, gazing through the window. Liz's soft-soled shoes were noiseless on the marble mosaic floor and she coughed to reveal her presence. The girl turned slowly, her dark eyes full of hatred as they swept over Liz from head to foot.

'Where's Nigel?' she rasped before Liz could speak. 'Where is he, I say?'

'I believe Nikos told you that Nigel's away.' Moving over to the sofa, Liz made a gesture with her hand. 'Won't you sit down?'

'*You* asking *me* to sit down! Do you know who I am?'

'Perhaps you'll enlighten me?'

The girl seethed. She came close to Liz, her eyes dark pools of wrath.

'Nigel and I were practically engaged before he went to England just over a week ago! What's happened? Who are you?'

'Engaged?' Liz glanced sceptically at her, recalling Nigel's words when she, Liz, had said she always swore never to give up her freedom.

'Strangely, so I did,' had been the response . . .

'Yes – engaged! Who are you?' the girl repeated aggressively. 'What's your name?'

Points of blue ice glittered in Liz's eyes.

'Mrs. Shapani,' she murmured spitefully. 'What's yours?'

The girl gritted her teeth.

'Sheldon!' She paced about for a second or two and

then sat down on the sofa. Liz herself took a chair and asked if she could get her visitor some refreshment.

'I want nothing from you! When will Nigel be back?'

'I've no idea.'

The admission was voiced before Liz realized what it meant. Greta looked up, an odd expression in her eyes.

'You've no idea? And newly married? How very strange.'

'I expect Nigel will phone me.' There was no response from Greta, who had suddenly become lost in thought. 'Why haven't you called before?' asked Liz curiously at length. 'We came home on Tuesday.'

'I was away myself. I arrived back only this morning and heard of Nigel's marriage. My maid's the sister of Nikos,' she added with impatience as Liz looked interrogatingly at her. 'She told me. I couldn't believe it – *I could not believe it!*' She glared at Liz with a black venom. 'I don't know what this is all about, or why he married you, but I know he can't possibly love you!'

Colour spread over Liz's cheeks and her impulse was to have her visitor shown out, but she was curious. This girl was beautiful, and from a man's view, thought Liz, extremely desirable. She was very dark, with big alluring eyes and the sort of lips men like to kiss. Her shape too, was more rounded than that of Liz – and Liz had often heard the crude expression that men 'prefer a little flesh on their women'.

'You told Nikos you wished to see me,' said Liz after a pause. 'If you will come to the point . . .?'

'I just wanted to look at you, that's all,' returned Greta insolently. 'I couldn't believe in your existence, even though my maid has never lied to me.' A small hesitation and then, 'Why did he marry you?'

Liz was facing the window and her attention was

caught by the sun glinting on the heights of Parnassus. Every hour the scene out there changed, even though the imperishable beauty of the mountain itself was ever the same.

'There is usually only one reason for marriage,' said Liz coldly at last.

'Usually, yes.' Greta's lips pursed. 'He went to England on other business altogether.'

Other business ... How much had he told this girl? Liz wondered and said with a hint of caution,

'You know what that business was, apparently?'

The other girl flushed and Liz shot her a perceptive glance.

'Nigel – er – he didn't have time to tell me about it.'

A faint smile hovered on Liz's mouth for a space.

'Perhaps,' she suggested quietly, 'he didn't wish to confide in you?'

Greta's eyes flashed angrily.

'I said he didn't have time! Nigel always confides in me! We were almost engaged – I've already told you that!' She stood up, and the hand holding her bag was tightly clenched about the handle. Liz surprised herself by feeling a strange pity for the girl. Nigel had obviously played about with her affections, and although Liz could never like the girl, feeling that this type asked for trouble, she at the same time found Nigel's conduct thoroughly heartless and inexcusable. 'I'll ring every single day – to find out when he'll be back!' Greta strode to the door and opened it before Liz could do so. 'I'll know what this is all about! He's not treating me like this and getting away with it!'

For a long while after the girl's departure Liz dwelt on the conversation. Nigel had told Greta he was going to England on business – which Liz supposed was correct, and yet ... A frown settled on her brow. Business ...

Somehow, that word was not quite the right one with which to describe the mission on which Nigel had gone to England.

'I'm splitting hairs,' said Liz to herself, and dismissed the matter from her mind.

With lunch over Liz decided to spend the afternoon in the shady courtyard, with a book. But the June day was hot and sultry and she stripped off, wearing only a brief pair of shorts and an even briefer covering at the top.

During the afternoon she had a visit from a distant cousin of Nigel's. Nikos brought him into the courtyard, having informed him of Nigel's absence, but saying Mrs. Nigel was in.

'*Mrs.* Nigel!' Liz heard him ejaculate as she glanced up from her book. 'What did you say, Nikos!'

'Mr. Nigel – he go to England, and return with a wife – Mrs. Nigel, this is your cousin, Mr. Spiros.'

The stocky young man just stared and stared, and Liz flushed, wishing she'd had time to go indoors for a more adequate covering. She did not mind this attire in her own country, but during her previous visit to Greece she had learned that a good deal of embarrassment could be avoided by concealing most of her body from the interested eyes of the Greek male.

'Won't you sit down?' she invited calmly at last, but Spiros still stood there, amazement on his handsome brown face. Nikos grinned and went off. He at least was deriving entertainment from these odd circumstances.

'Are you Nigel's wife?' inquired Spiros, sitting down in a dazed sort of way on the wicker chair opposite to Liz. 'Am I dreaming?'

She had to laugh, so comical he looked.

'I'm Nigel's wife, yes. We've been married almost a week now.'

'But – but—' He stared again – and she re-opened her book and spread it on her lap. 'Nigel – married! He'll never get married—I mean – are you sure?' he then asked, regarding her with extreme suspicion.

'Would Nikos lie?'

'No . . . but— I still can't take it in! I mean, who are you? I've never even heard of you. Have you and Nigel known each other long? And where did you meet? He hasn't visited England for years until last week.'

She hesitated. How much did Nigel intend telling his relatives?

'Nigel and I haven't known each other very long,' she began, when rather to her relief Spiros interrupted her, suddenly becoming aware of his lack of grace and courtesy, characteristics which as a Greek he considered of prime importance.

'I say, I'm awfully sorry, but I haven't welcomed you to Kastri, nor even asked your name. I'm Spiros, as you've heard. Spiros Loukia.'

'How do you do,' she smiled. 'My name's Elizabeth. I'm afraid I always get called Liz.'

'Liz . . .' He thought about it. 'I like it. Liz, you are welcome to Kastri!'

'Thank you. ' Liz smiled again, taking in the dark hair and eyes, the fleshy mouth, and the typical high cheekbones of the Greek. 'What refreshment can I offer you?' She wasn't yet able to clap her hands for Nikos and as she had no intention of getting up she merely looked around, hoping he might be somewhere about.

'A long drink. Lemonade or something.'

'I'll have the same. I don't see Nikos. Would you mind going into the house and telling him what we want?'

Spiros looked questioningly at her and clapped his hands. Nikos appeared at once and the drinks were

46

brought out, Nikos placing a small table between Liz and her companion.

'Will you tell Maria to bring me out a wrap?' asked Liz as Nikos moved away.

'Certainly, Mrs. Nigel.'

'And now,' said Spiros as he took up his glass, 'how about satisfying your new cousin's curiosity and telling him all about it?' Having accepted the fact of her marriage Spiros now evinced no further surprise and added, before she could speak, 'I never thought Nigel would fall like that – all of a rush, as you might say – but, Liz, looking at you I can see he hadn't a chance!'

She took that unsmilingly. Flattery was neither desired nor appreciated by Liz. Men's opinions of her were of no consequence. In fact, she would prefer them to keep those opinions to themselves, no matter how complimentary they might be. Nevertheless, after a moment she talked to him in a friendly way, saying it was a whirlwind courtship and that she and Nigel had married in haste because he had his business to attend to and it would have been inconvenient for him to make another trip to England. Liz stopped to take the wrap from Maria and put it on. She felt more at ease now she was covered.

'Well,' said Spiros, 'it's certainly romantic.' An odd little pause and then, hesitantly, 'You haven't met – er – a girl called Greta yet?'

She had to smile then.

'As a matter of fact, I have.' She went on to tell Spiros about the visit, her smile broadening as she watched his changing expression.

'There'll be trouble with that one,' he declared when she stopped speaking. 'She became so possessive, and it was clear that she expected the affair to develop into something permanent, but she's lived here long enough to

47

know that Greeks never marry their pillow friends.' He stopped then, and flushed, and a little laugh escaped Liz as she perceived his consternation.

'Don't look like that. I don't mind about Greta.'

'You don't? But then the English are broad-minded about these things. Never fear, though, Liz, he'll be finished with her now.'

Liz didn't care whether he had or not, but naturally she kept that to herself. She mused for a space on the situation and saw no reason at all why Nigel should finish with Greta. He would probably explain why he'd had to marry; Greta would accept that it was a necessity, and on learning there was nothing between Liz and her husband she would almost certainly agree to carry on in the same old way. That would suit Liz. For the memory of that kiss and that ardent embrace was still with her. She wouldn't care for any nonsense of *that* sort to enter her husband's head.

'Where does Greta live?' Liz asked curiously. 'Does she work at all?'

'She lives here in Kastri – or Delphi, as most of us call it. Her father was employed on antiquities, but he's retired now. Greta acts as a guide now and then – at the Sanctuary over there. She and her parents aren't short of money. An uncle died last year and left them pretty well off. I think Greta does this guiding merely as a diversion.'

'Has – has she been friendly with Nigel for long?'

'A couple of years. Nigel's stuck to her longer than most—' He stopped, dismayed, then he gave a shrug of resignation. 'I'm a big idiot! – but it's too late now to undo it. Nigel's been a bit of a rake, but don't worry, Liz – *please* don't worry,' he emphasized, looking anxiously at her. 'Nigel's not the man to be unfaithful. You won't worry? Do say you won't.'

Her eyes lit with amusement. If only he knew!

'I won't worry,' she promised.

'And you won't tell Nigel I made that slip?'

'I'll not say a word.'

As the afternoon wore on Liz and Spiros seemed very quickly to get to know one another, and to her surprise she found herself enjoying his company. He was gay and witty, and he was informative, telling her about the Sanctuary and the surrounding districts. She must certainly go to Amphissa, and to Itea – and he himself would be more than willing to take her should Nigel be away on business, which he often was, it seemed.

'You'll come with me?'

Trips of this nature would provide diversions in the monotony of her life, she decided, and said yes, she would go with him.

It was as he was about to leave that Spiros mentioned the will, asking Liz if she had heard about it. She became cagey, feigning puzzlement without actually saying anything.

Spiros then told her all about the will of Nigel's great-grandfather, telling Liz how it was interdependent on that of another old man. He mentioned the broken engagement of her sister and finally he did say something which brought Liz forward in her chair, her blue eyes widening with interest.

'Nigel's known all along that those wills were invalid, because his lawyer told him so. The two men were millionaires, and they were very old when they changed their wills, being influenced by this stupid Fellowship – which was no more than a band of cranks. When Nigel's great-grandfather died Nigel was all set to contest the will, but his lawyer advised him to wait until the other man died as the case would have more strength if the two families fought the wills together, and as Nigel's almost a millionaire himself he naturally wasn't in a hurry, so he took his lawyer's advice and waited. However, when the second old man died there didn't seem to be any point in contesting the wills because the clause I spoke about was complied with – as I've mentioned – by the engagement of this Vivien with Nigel's half-brother. But this Vivien found she didn't want to marry Arthur after all, so last week Nigel went to England to talk with this other family and arrange with them to contest both wills together. It would be a walk-over, Nigel's lawyer said, and the wills would without doubt be declared null and void.'

As he proceeded with his narrative Liz felt she should break in, to inform Spiros who she was, but she refrained, too curious to interrupt. And even when he had stopped speaking she still remained silent, reflecting on that scene at the Hall when Nigel had taken over as it were and gone round all the family, suggesting marriages which he knew could not possibly take place . . . until at last he came to Liz and himself. Liz now realized why she had been unable to accept the word 'business' to describe Nigel's mission. For his mission – so Liz had then supposed – was merely to discover what had gone wrong between Vivien and Arthur, and endeavour to put it right. But he had not come on a mission at all. He had come, as he had obviously told Greta, on business – the business of setting in motion a lawsuit which would result in those two wills being quashed.

Liz's eyes flickered with perception. Nigel must have wanted to marry her!

After coming to England for the express purpose of having those wills nullified he had suddenly changed his mind and decided to marry Liz. Yes, he had actually *wanted* to marry her. There was no other explanation, because Nigel was possessed of the knowledge that a marriage was in fact unnecessary. For some reason of his own Nigel had forced her into marriage. Liz's rising anger began to possess her whole body. Forced into marriage! What a fool she had been. Where was her own intelligence? She also should have perceived at once that those two wills would never be upheld in a court. They were too ridiculous – yes, she could see this now – the testators having in their dotage been influenced by the Fellowship – an organization which had often provided copy for derisive, fun-poking newspapermen.

Forced into an unnecessary marriage ... and because of some whim of Nigel's! Liz's fists clenched and her nostrils quivered. She could at that moment have struck her husband dead without a moment's compunction. If only he were here! But wait ... he would learn a thing or two about her temper.

Nigel was away for ten days; Greta rang every day as threatened, but after the third day Liz lost patience and gave Nikos instructions to answer the phone. He looked oddly at Liz, as well he might, but she disregarded his stare – and the faint glimmer of amusement in his eyes. By this time she supposed Greta's maid, having been put in possession of the fact that Liz occupied a single room, had duly passed on the information to her mistress, with the result that Greta must now be even more at a loss as to why her lover had married.

Liz was out when Nigel returned, having gone into the village to buy one or two small gifts to send to her family. She also had a wedding-present to buy for Vivien, but she found nothing in Kastri and decided to wait until she went down to Athens, she and Spiros having decided to make the trip at the end of the month, when he had a few days' holiday. They would stay overnight, for the journey was too long and tiring to make in one day.

On seeing the car standing on the wide forecourt Liz felt a sudden surge of fury that threatened to consume her whole body.

'Hello,' was Nigel's greeting as she came on to the patio where he was seated, drinking coffee. '*Yassoo!*'

She glowered at him, her eyes points of flint.

'Perhaps you'll explain,' she said without preamble, 'the reason why you tricked me into marriage?'

The merest silence and then, calmly,

'Do you mind being a little more explicit?' Picking up his coffee cup, Nigel took a drink and returned the cup to its saucer.

'Your cousin Spiros called!' she snapped. 'He told me that you've always been aware of the invalidity of those wills! Explain, if you please, the reason for our marriage!' Her voice had built up to a crescendo and it did nothing for her temper to see a pained and rather irritated expression appear on Nigel's face. And he frowned at her as he said,

'I'm not deaf, girl. Kindly speak more quietly – and more slowly – when addressing me.' He looked her over, his green eyes coldly searching. 'You appear to be losing control. This in a woman I cannot abide, and the sooner you learn to practise calm the better it will suit me. I noticed a similar lack of control in your attitude towards your sister,' he added censoriously, seeming quite unaware of the rise of dark crimson in her cheeks and the quivering movement of her nostrils. 'If you expect to have my attention then sit down and relate to me, rationally, what Spiros has said to you.'

Liz pressed her teeth together; the grating sound was heard by Nigel and his eyes glinted, then measured her

52

darkly. If only she had his man's strength! If only she could strike a blow that would knock him to the ground!

'I've just told you Spiros said you'd always known those wills would never hold in a court. You came to England for the specific purpose of seeing me – or some member of my family – to discuss the wills, with a view to contesting them.' She moved closer so that she could look down at him instead of across at him. The gesture was not lost on Nigel and, had Liz known him better, she would have been duly warned by the haughty raising of those straight black brows. But as yet she and her husband were strangers and Liz continued, sublimely unaware of the exception Nigel had taken to her action, 'What made you change your mind – I demand to know? I demand to know why I find myself married to you when I could have been free!' Her voice vibrated with emotion – and it was still louder than it should be. Nigel pointed to a chair.

'Sit down,' he commanded, and Liz gaped at him, dumbfounded by his order.

'I shall not!' Sit down ...! Who did he think he was ordering about? But she instinctively took a few backward steps as Nigel rose from his chair and purposefully advanced upon her. Without giving her time to grasp his intention he lifted her off her feet and dumped her, none too gently, into the chair. Almost suffocating with fury, Liz instinctively made to rise, but Nigel's hand, betraying by its pressure the powerful strength of its owner, kept her where she was.

'Take care, Liz,' came the soft, animal-like warning. 'I told you I was neither a tolerant man nor an easy-going one. Try my patience too far and you might find yourself nursing a bruise or two.'

'A – a—?' Liz stared up at him unbelievingly. 'Wh –

what did you say?' It wasn't possible, she told herself; this couldn't be happening to her – whose will and strength of character had always been so formidable that people thought twice before trying to oppose any law she might choose to make. At the Hall she had ruled them all; whatever she said went – without argument. Only Vivien had at last defied her, and for the first time in her life Liz had experienced defeat.

Well, she decided, grinding her teeth, she had no intention of experiencing defeat for a second time – especially at the hands of this heathen whom she had disliked excessively from the very moment of setting eyes on him at the fair. And she hadn't forgiven or forgotten that kiss, which insulted; nor that unnecessary show of strength simply because she had resented the insult and tried to break away from his embrace. He had deliberately fettered her in hawsers of steel – just to demonstrate how puny were her efforts at freeing herself.

'You heard me.' That lazy drawl now as Nigel sat down in his chair, his eyes never leaving her face. Move, that expression warned, and she would very soon regret it. 'Now, if you're prepared to speak coherently I'm ready to listen—'

'You're not talking to a child!' she interrupted, sending him a savage glance. 'And I did *not* speak incoherently!'

Nigel drew an impatient breath, then said,

'What's the matter with you? It may interest you to know that up till now I've led a peaceful, well-organized life—'

'Then you should have kept it peaceful and well-organized – and steered clear of me! I've asked you why you married me!'

'You know why I married you.'

She glared at him.

'Are you denying your original intention was to contest your great-grandfather's will?'

He frowned at that and said impatiently,

'Spiros talks too much. And it wouldn't be so bad if he knew what he was talking about.'

'He—?' she looked suspiciously at him. 'Don't try to hoodwink me at this late stage! You must have informed Spiros of your confidence over that will. Why did you decide on marriage,' she cried, 'when the simplest way was to follow your original plan and contest the will? What made you change your mind?'

'The simplest way was not the contesting of the will,' he returned quietly, ignoring her last question. 'The simplest way was the one I chose – marriage.' He stopped, a sardonic light entering his eyes as he looked her over. 'I'm thinking already that I've made a blunder—'

'Thinking?' Her brows shot up. 'You can be *sure* you have. For some reason of your own you changed your mind about contesting the will and chose marriage with me instead – but you'll live to regret it, I can assure you! Before I've finished with you you'll wish you'd never set eyes on me!'

His jaw flexed.

'I've warned you to be careful,' he reminded her softly.

'You've tricked me. Do you expect me to accept that without any complaint? I'm not one of your docile Greek women!'

'It isn't necessary to tell me that,' he retorted, not without a touch of humour. 'Unless my eyes deceive me those fists of yours are just itching to find a target.'

'How right you are,' she quivered. 'Nothing would give me greater satisfaction than to knock you off that chair!'

'I'm sure it wouldn't.' A lean brown hand was negligently raised as Nigel stifled a yawn. 'However, I'm sure you're far too wise to run your head into danger.'

'I'm not afraid of danger,' she challenged, her eyes blue sparks of militance. 'So don't be too sure I'll avoid it.'

Once more he gave an impatient intake of his breath, appearing bored all at once and irritated by the conversation.

'Liz,' he said in a softly-threatening tone, 'I keep on proffering advice and you seem intent on ignoring it. But I'm not a man to waste words – and I really think that, for your own good, you should heed my advice. As I've said, my life hitherto has been lived peaceably, and I'm having no female—'

'Don't call me a female!'

He raised his brows with feigned surprise, then laughed as Liz flushed and looked away.

'May I divert for a moment,' he remarked affably, 'to say you're one of the most attractive females I've ever yet set eyes on? – though don't let that go to your head,' he added swiftly, still amused by the fact of her refusing to meet his gaze. 'Because I have met some ravishing females in my time, and you win only by a short head—'

'Are you bragging of your conquests?' she queried with contempt. 'Or your profligacy?'

'Is there a difference?' he laughed, and then, after a moment's thought, 'Perhaps there is a subtle one. However, to revert to what I was saying: I'll have no female working herself up into a towering rage with me and getting away with it.' He wagged a forefinger at her, just as if she were a small child. Liz felt like snapping off one of the bamboo canes and rapping that finger good and hard. 'So

I'm recommending you to curb that disgusting temper, for otherwise you'll be involved in a clash you won't forget in a hurry.' So soft, that indolent drawl, yet deeply threatening. Unable to speak for the wrath which choked her, Liz decided to go into the house, but much to her chagrin she felt half-afraid of standing up, in case he should decide on another display of his mastery. And after a while she did manage to calm down sufficiently to question him again about the marriage.

'I've already told you,' he frowned. 'It was the simplest way.'

'You said you didn't really need the money,' she reminded him.

'I believe I did say something of the kind,' he admitted. 'But I also said it was a shame to lose so large a fortune.'

'You're prevaricating,' she snapped, frustrated by the knowledge that she was to remain unenlightened as to the reason for Nigel's decision not to contest the will.

'Am I?' He looked at her and through her, with that air of boredom about him which irritated her even more than his arrogance. 'Shall we let the matter drop, Liz?' and, when she would have interrupted him, 'We *will* let the matter drop.' And then, after a small thoughtful silence, he veered the subject, asking what Liz had told Spiros by way of an explanation of their marriage.

'I kept in mind what you said about our being amicable before your friends,' she told him after a pettish moment during which she searched unsuccessfully for an answer that would give him the headache he deserved. 'And so he has no idea that this isn't a – a normal marriage. He doesn't know I'm in any way connected with the will.'

'It was very wise of you to keep our secret, Liz.' He looked squarely at her. 'Remember to keep it – always, because if you don't you'll answer to me.'

CHAPTER FOUR

LATER in the day Liz was on the lawn, sunbathing, and still inwardly fuming at Nigel's firm evasion, when she heard the phone ring, and immediately it stopped Nigel's voice reached her from the house.

Greta, in all probability, and Liz was tempted to enter the house by one of the french windows, and listen to the conversation. However, the idea of eavesdropping was anything but attractive and after some deliberation she lay down again, rolling over on her stomach so as to tan evenly. To her surprise Nigel appeared and she realized that had she decided to listen she would not have had time to do so.

'Was that your lady-friend?' she couldn't resist saying and Nigel, about to walk past her, halted abruptly. Liz brought her head up, undaunted by his arrogant expression.

'Explain that question,' he snapped, tensely impatient.

'She called on me a couple of days after you left. She seemed terribly upset about our marriage.'

He frowned.

'How the devil did she come to hear of it?' He spoke softly, to himself, and Liz only just caught the words.

'Servants,' she returned briefly, and Nigel nodded his head in a grim sort of way. He looked down at Liz. She was as scantily-clad as on the occasion of his cousin's visit, but as she intended taking advantage of the sun she had decided she must acquire an immunity to the stares of any Greek male who happened to see her.

'You had a conversation with Greta? Why didn't you mention it earlier?'

'We didn't have much opportunity of discussing your amours,' she rejoined tartly, deriving intense satisfaction from the sudden glint of anger which entered his eyes. 'We were concerned with a much less pleasant matter!'

His eyes raked her figure – and for some reason she could not explain Liz swung quickly over on to her back. The action brought a smile of sardonic amusement to her husband's lips before he moved away, making for the gate leading out of the grounds. Liz followed his tall figure till it was lost, wondering where he was going. To Greta's? Why should she waste her time pondering on his movements? They could never be of interest to her, just as hers could never be of interest to him.

Why had he married her? Liz asked herself again, at the same time shrugging angrily because she felt she would never find an answer to the question. What a provocatively obstinate man he was! – deliberately forcing her into marriage and then refusing to say why. Spiros did not know what he was talking about, Nigel had implied, but Liz felt sure Spiros spoke the truth. With the possibility of a broken engagement between his half-brother and Vivien, Nigel had decided the wills must be contested, and the arranging of this was the sole purpose of his visit to England. Musing on this for a long while, an idea suddenly occurred to Liz which made her sit up with a jerk, her blue eyes opening very wide. Could it possibly be that the kiss had given Nigel an appetite for more ...? There was no doubt that he thoroughly enjoyed that kiss ... *and* the feel of her body against him, judging by the almost primitive way in which he held her. She had speculated on whether his motive in suggesting marriage had stemmed from desire, Liz recalled, and now, as she sat there, in the sun, with peace all round and only the murmur of insects to break the vast silence, she experienced a tinge of apprehension. Supposing Nigel should decide to ...? But he'd supplied her with her own bedroom. Had *that* been his intention then surely he would have arranged things differently right from the start.

Impatient, and still slightly apprehensive, Liz got up and went into the house to get dressed.

On coming out of her bedroom into the hall she heard the phone ring and went to answer it.

'Nigel,' came the harsh voice from over the line. 'Where is he?'

'My husband's out. Can I take a message?'

'I phoned earlier and told him I wished to see him. Why hasn't he come?' Liz held the phone away from her ear. So Nigel had not gone to see Greta. Liz smiled faintly. If Greta had spoken to him in this manner Liz could very well understand why he hadn't. 'Where is he?' Greta's voice was now high-pitched and shrill. '*Where is he?*'

'I'm afraid I couldn't say where he is,' returned Liz at length. 'Would you like me to give him a message?' she asked again.

A small silence. Liz could fairly see the anger on Greta's face.

'Yes. You can tell him I'll be calling on him this evening—' She broke off, then Liz heard a very different tone as Greta said, 'Nigel – you've come! Nigel, why did you ...?' Another silence and then the receiver clicked. Liz replaced hers, allowing herself a satisfied little smile. She had no need to worry about Nigel's amorous tendencies. Greta would satisfy those, as she had done for the past two years – or so Spiros implied.

Spiros called later and Liz invited him to stay to tea.

'Where's Nigel?' Spiros asked on first approaching Liz from the terrace fronting the house. 'I know he's back; Mother saw him in his car.'

Some mischief entered into Liz and she said,

'He's gone to see his girl-friend.'

'He's—?' Spiros stared for a moment and then shrugged. 'Yes, I suppose he had to. I wonder how she'll take it – being thrown over, I mean?' There was a malicious note in his voice which made it clear that Greta had never been popular with Spiros.

'Perhaps,' murmured Liz as they sat down at the table, 'she won't be thrown over.'

'She'll cling to Nigel, you mean?' Spiros shook his head. 'You've not known Nigel very long – but you must have learned enough to be sure that if he intends throwing Greta over then she'll be thrown over.'

'He might not intend throwing her over.' The words were out before Liz realized it and she searched her companion's face to see what effect they had on him. That he was both amazed and puzzled was evident. He seemed to deliberate on her suggestion for a long while before he spoke.

'Of course he'll throw her over—' Spiros looked at her, a frown on his brow. 'You're so calm about Greta. Aren't English women jealous? A Greek woman would rave and storm if she knew her husband had gone to see his ex-pillow friend.'

Liz hesitated. Immersed as she was in anger against her husband she would dearly have loved to give rein to her spite and tell Spiros the whole story, but of course she refrained. If she forgot to keep their secret she would answer to him, Nigel had said, and much as she would have liked to ignore that warning, Liz felt her nerves must assuredly suffer from a prolonged campaign of discord with her husband.

'I haven't a jealous disposition,' she offered at last, aware of Spiros's continued stare of puzzlement and interrogation. No more was said about the matter, for at that moment Nigel appeared, striding across the lawn like some magnificent deity of a long departed age. His slim body moved with the sort of smooth rhythm one would associate with wings; his face carried the sculptured lines so magnificently portrayed in the face of Apollo himself. Behind Nigel rose the perpendicular walls of the Phaedriades in all their harsh, convulsed splendour. The vast unreal silence of this sacred place affected Liz's senses and in spite of her thorough dislike of the man she found her imagination stimulated in a way that could only be described as flattering to him. A figure out of place in this mundane world, he seemed, his long arms swinging, his black hair tousled slightly and falling on to his low aristocratic brow. No doubt about it, there was a certain peerless nobility about him which Liz had never before encountered in a man. He would look more at home on Olympus – among the gods, she thought, her mind wandering, out of control for a space as she imagined him as a lover. Masterful and demanding, he would make no attempt to curb his primitive instincts – or even to temper them by the application of a little finesse ... or would he? After all, he was no novice, apparently— Colouring to the roots at her thoughts, Liz shut them off, lowering her head as her husband reached the patio and took the three steps in one easy graceful leap. He was looking at her, she sensed it, but dared not raise her head until her face had cooled.

Nigel sat down; the two men began to talk, Spiros wanting to know all about the marriage and saying how surprised they all were – the aunts and uncles and cousins, including those several times removed. Nigel was friendly but non-committal and presently Spiros gave up. Nigel, Liz soon gathered, was a law unto himself and although some of his actions might surprise his relatives and friends, they were accepted with resignation, and any criticisms or comments were kept from Nigel's ears.

Nigel clapped his hands imperiously and Nikos appeared.

'Bring me some tea,' Nigel ordered, leaning back in his chair and regarding his wife's bent head inscrutably. She glanced up, hoping her colour had returned to normal. She was in a gay cotton dress, low at the neck and full-skirted. Her hair was a cloud of gold and silver, framing a face that had turned heads ever since Liz could remember. But flattering glances fell away unheeded, and the fact that she had been described as 'too tough to handle' troubled her not at all. On the contrary, she was rather proud of the fact that men fought shy of her, and had scoffed on that one occasion when a discouraged suitor had roundly declared that the day would dawn when she would meet her match.

'I hope I'm around when that happens!' was his final bitter comment.

Liz had laughed in sheer amusement. This one had tried so very hard to arouse in her some pliancy and feminine softness, but like the rest he had failed utterly.

'Then you'll have to stay around for a long while,' was her confident and heartless retort.

Nigel continued to stare at her, then his gaze wandered and he took in every graceful line and curve of her body. She flushed again and his eyes flicked her face with taunting amusement. Her mouth went tight. Control was difficult, for her temper was unpredictable at the best of times. If only Spiros had not been present she would have told Nigel in no uncertain terms to keep his mocking glances to himself!

However, Spiros was there and after the three had been engaged in a casual conversation for a short while Spiros mentioned the projected trip to Athens. At this Nigel's eyes flickered in the oddest way, and unaccountably Liz felt a sudden stir of uneasiness.

'You've arranged to go to Athens together ... and stay overnight?'

'That's right. I thought you'd still be away, but it won't matter, will it? – unless you want to come too,' added Spiros as an afterthought, and his cousin's black brows lifted a fraction.

'Thanks for the invitation,' he retorted, leaning away from the table as Nikos appeared with the tea-tray.

Spiros looked slightly put out then, becoming faintly apologetic.

'Have I said something I shouldn't? I mean, there's no harm in Liz and me going to Athens, is there? We *are* cousins.'

Liz was watching Nigel intently. Why the proprietorial manner all at once? Why should he care where she went – or with whom? It was none of his business, anyway.

'Of course there's no harm in our going to Athens together,' she said in firm and even tones. And she added, simply because she had to, 'Nigel's just as broad-minded as I am—' She smiled at him with a sort of acid sweetness. 'Aren't you – dear?'

An almost imperceptible sound reached her ears and she could scarcely contain her laughter as she realized Nigel was gritting his teeth.

Ignoring her question he said, in a very soft tone,

'I hate to be a spoil-sport, but I can't have my wife

running all over Athens with my bachelor cousin.' He flicked a sideways glance at Liz and added, 'It just isn't done in my country – and Spiros is well aware of that.'

'No such thing!' objected Spiros with some indignation. 'It is done – with relations.'

'With relations, perhaps.'

'Isn't Liz a relation?'

'Undoubtedly – but not sufficiently close for the kind of trip you were planning.'

Liz flushed angrily. Impossible to retaliate with Spiros's being here, and Nigel knew this. All she could do was to send him a speaking glance – from which, to her added annoyance, he appeared to derive some considerable amusement. How, wondered Liz clenching her fists unconsciously, was she going to tolerate this insufferable man for the rest of her life?

'You're serious, Nigel?' Spiros looked disbelievingly at his cousin. 'We're staying only the one night—'

'Liz is not going with you to Athens,' his cousin cut in with crisp finality. 'Let's hear no more about it!' He poured himself a cup of tea and leant back in his chair with it, deliberately avoiding Liz's eyes. This threatened to spark off her smouldering anger, but she somehow managed to contain herself until the departure of their visitor.

'And now,' began Liz almost before Spiros was out of earshot, 'perhaps you'll explain! The arrangement was that both you and I go our own ways. I'm not interfering with you, and I'll thank you not to interfere with me. I'll go out with whom I like!'

'It so happens,' said Nigel helping himself to a sandwich, 'that I've invited some friends to dinner on Saturday evening. Naturally you will have to be at home.'

She glanced suspiciously at him.

'I'm not at all sure I believe that.'

'You're saying I'm a liar?' Nigel's tones were dangerously quiet.

'I believe you just thought it up on the spur of the moment – so you'd have an excuse for objecting to my going away with Spiros.'

'An excuse isn't necessary. If I say you're not going away with Spiros then you don't go. And that's what I am saying – you *don't go*!'

'I—!' Black rage seized her. Clear-headed thinking was totally submerged by it and wild unconsidered words tumbled from her quivering lips. 'You dare to attempt to give *me* orders! I'm neither your subjugated wife nor your eager willing mistress! If you want to tyrannize over someone then go to *her*! Doubtless she thoroughly enjoys being bullied, otherwise she wouldn't be so anxious to keep you!'

An awful silence followed, the freezing chill of her husband's rising fury affected Liz in spite of herself and involuntarily she shrank back in her chair. Slowly and deliberately Nigel placed his cup and saucer on the table and, with the same unhurried deliberation, he rose and moved round the table to stand looking down at her for a long and dangerous moment. And then with a lightning move he had her on her feet and she was shaken until the blood pounded in her head.

'Speak to me like that again and you'll be black and blue.' His voice was surprisingly quiet – but awesomely so. White lines of anger had crept under the tan of his face and his eyes were hard as serpentine. 'In my country a woman respects her husband – and it's my intention that you shall learn to respect me!' Releasing her, he at the same time gave her a thrust which sent her staggering back into her chair, her heartbeats wildly out of control. 'I've a good mind to insist on an apology.' He remained standing over her, his expression one of indecision. This was too much for Liz and she just had to say, her voice high-pitched with fury,

'You can dismiss the idea at once, for you'll get no apology from me!'

His eyes glinted, he looked like Satan himself, thought Liz, and wondered why she had been so foolish as to marry him. But on entering into the contract she had had no notion he would act in this unpredictable way. The marriage, a purely mercenary contrivance, would leave them both practically unaffected. Of necessity she must live in his country, but that was all ... or at least Liz had believed that would be all. Why this assumption of mastery? She would learn to respect him, he asserted – and he meant it too, Liz had no illusions about that. She never would respect him, of course, but undoubtedly Nigel believed he could coerce her into doing so.

Moving away at last, Nigel sat down.

'I warned you, right at the beginning, to take care.' The indolent drawl which had so irritated her on several previous occasions now replaced the cold fury in his voice and he leant back, his immaculate white linen shirt contrasting with the dark blue covering of the garden chair in which he sat. 'I might as well give you an extra word of warning, Liz,' he added, casting her a sideways glance which greatly increased her irritation. 'This is that nothing would afford me greater satisfaction than to chasten you by physical force, it's always having been my firm conviction that women, like animals should be beaten into submission—' He broke off, laughing at her expression. For undoubtedly it did seem that Liz would go off into a convulsion, judging by the purple tinge creeping into her cheeks, and the slow spasmodic clenching and unclenching of her hands. And yet through the haze of dark venom possessing her she sensed he was not quite as serious as he would have her believe. Was he deriving fun at her expense? Liz ground her teeth and said in a suffocated voice,

'I don't quite know what you're about, but if you continue this little game you're playing—'

'Game?' Nigel quirked an eyebrow at her. 'My dear Liz, I assure you I'm in no mood for playing games. Never in my life have I been more in earnest. Either you learn to act as a woman and not as a shrew, or you take the consequences which,' he added in accents softer and more emphatic, 'will, I assure you, be far from pleasant.'

She stared at him, thankfully aware of the calmer, more even rhythm of her heartbeats. His strength, she had previously owned, was not a thing to be scorned, and despite the fury which still possessed her she made a mental vow to practise a little discretion in future, for she had no desire to find herself subjected to another exhibition of his violence.

Liz continued to hold his gaze. He puzzled her intensely, this man who, having travelled to England for the express purpose of contesting his great-grandfather's will, had changed his mind, for no apparent reason, and, quite unnecessarily, chosen to marry her. Marriage ... it was so important a step to take, just like that, without thought. And being half Greek, and a member of the Greek Orthodox Church, he knew that on taking that momentous step he was binding himself for life to Liz, knew he would never be free again and that should he ever meet someone with whom he could fall in love his life would be ruined. Yes, his behaviour had been most odd indeed, mused Liz, sensing a mystery more acutely than ever. This man was certainly an enigma to her. She sighed at last and said, without much hope of receiving a satisfactory reply,

'Do you mind explaining what this is all about? It would appear on the surface that your objective is to – er – reform me, and I'm most interested to discover the reason.'

Nigel flashed her an amused glance.

'So you agree you need reforming? Well, that's something; perhaps my task will not be so difficult after all. It's half the battle that you're aware of your shortcomings—' His lips quivered at her explosive expression. He was so cool now, so maddeningly superior as he sat there, in that attitude of indolence, gazing at her through half-closed eyes.

Liz's own eyes narrowed. Just what was his little game? Could it be that these attempts to master her were conducted merely for a diversion? From what Liz could deduce his life was sufficiently full; he had his business, being one of the largest tobacco growers in Greece, and he had Greta ... Why, then, waste time on his wife?

Suddenly Liz decided the most effective way to combat this man was to disregard his endeavours, to keep her temper in check and display a complete lack of interest in his threats. And yet, because she was Liz, and had never been mastered in her life nor even given an order, for that matter, she just had to make some sort of reply to his impudent words.

'Undoubtedly you intend keeping me in ignorance as to the reason for this desire to change my character, but I do feel it's only fair to warn you you've set yourself an impossible task.'

'Think so?' quizzically. 'Time will tell, my dear, whether or not I've set myself an impossible task.' Liz searched for something to say, but she was unsuccessful, and after a while Nigel changed the subject, telling her about the friends he had invited to dinner on the coming Saturday evening. 'There are three couples, the men all being Greek, but two of the wives are English. The men are business associates of mine as well as friends, and I hope, Liz, that you'll oblige me by being the perfect hostess. You must have had plenty of experience – in your stately home in England,' he added. 'And I hope I shall have no complaints to voice when the evening comes to an end.'

'I might oblige,' she returned tartly, with the deliberate intention of being awkward, and Nigel flicked her a warning glance.

'You *will* oblige, Liz,' he told her softly.

'And if I don't?'

'Then you'll wish with all your heart you had,' Nigel calmly returned.

Liz leant back in her chair, herself calm now and greatly intrigued.

'These subtle threats—'

'There's nothing subtle about them, I assure you. If you're a sensible girl you'll guard against their being carried into effect.'

'Just what are you trying to do?'

Nigel threw her a faintly mocking glance.

'At the moment, just extending a timely warning.'

She was still intrigued and, somewhat to her disgust, interested. Never before had she met a man as tough as he. The men she had known had fallen, initially, for her looks, but on learning more of her formidable character each had made a rather hurried retreat. The one who had declared her to be too tough to handle had merely voiced the opinions of her other, more polite suitors. Faint humour lit her beautiful eyes as she mused on these hopefuls and suddenly she was acutely aware of her husband's gaze fixed intently upon her. She glanced across at him and for some indefinable reason a hint of colour rose to enhance the beauty of her face. She was in the shade of the vines sheltering the patio, but shafts of sunlight penetrated the foliage to embellish her hair with pure gold. The slow pulsating of a muscle in Nigel's neck caught her eyes and she glanced down. His shirt was open, just sufficiently for her to see the mahogany of his skin become lost beneath the mass of black hair on which lay a plain gold crucifix hanging from a slender chain. The crucifix surprised her, for although Liz knew he went to church she would not have thought he would wear a crucifix. Her gaze moved to his hand, resting in a negligent sort of way on the arm of the chair. The back of his hand was also covered with hair, as was his wrist and forearm. She raised her head; Nigel was regarding her with interest. The green eyes also held an odd expression in their depths.

'You puzzle me,' admitted Liz, drawn to speech because the silence was hanging uncomfortably between them. 'I must own I haven't ever met anyone quite like you.'

Nigel inclined his head in a gesture of surprise; obviously he had not expected such candour as this.

'Nor have I ever met anyone like you,' he returned on a faintly sardonic note. 'You intrigued me right from the start.'

Liz flushed, in memory living again through those moments of rage when he had imprisoned her and forced his vile and prolonged kiss upon her.

'I fail to see why I should have intrigued you,' she murmured at last, and there was a flash of white teeth as Nigel smiled.

71

'Don't dissimulate, Liz. You're fully aware that you're vastly different from the ordinary run of females.'

Despite herself she had to laugh.

'So we're two odd ones out?'

'Not necessarily.' And then, with a strange inflection in his voice, 'Like happens to have found like.'

Her eyes widened. That disturbing idea flashed through her mind again.

'Why did you marry me?' she demanded.

He merely shrugged and said,

'Why ask when you know? The marriage was one of convenience.'

Liz threw him a warning glance.

'Then see you keep it that way,' she said.

'Is it possible that I detect a shade of fear in your voice?' he inquired gently.

'Fear? Certainly not! What have I to fear?'

He looked at her, then spoke at length, his accents light and mocking.

'You are afraid, Liz, despite this show, afraid I might just decide to seduce you—' He broke off, laughing. 'No, that's not the right word, is it? After all, we are married.' He laughed again and his green eyes mocked as they rested on her face. 'How enchantingly you blush, my dear. You know, at times like this you are all woman – desirably feminine—'

'Cut it out!' she flashed, furious at her inability to control her fluctuating colour. 'Try any tricks and you'll receive a shock!'

'A shock?' Nigel raised his brows. 'That savours of a challenge, Liz – and I'm just the man to accept it.'

'You don't know my strength!'

His brows rose even higher.

'You haven't given me much of a display up till now.'

She knew he was thinking of that shaking he had just given her, and he was probably also recalling the incident of that kiss, when she had put up her futile struggles. A swift intake of her breath gave evidence of her fury and frustration. She turned away, wondering why she allowed this man to incense her like this, setting her emotions on fire. It wasn't as if he meant those subtle threats; they were voiced merely to infuriate her and, perhaps, to implant in her a feeling of apprehension. Aware of his steady gaze she was drawn irresistibly to meet it. But on noting the mocking amusement in his eyes she glanced swiftly away again, to where the cluster of hibiscus bushes marked the boundary of Nigel's land, beyond which spread the timeless Greek landscape, a landscape of deep unity yet of ceaseless variety. The fearsome gorge of the Pleistos falling away to the vast sea of olives that was the Sacred Plain of Amphissa; the contorted overthrust massif that partly girded it, while across the glittering aquamarine waters of the Corinthian Gulf could be discerned the snow-capped mountains of the Peloponnese.

The silence became oppressive and Liz stirred, a strange restlessness having taken possession of her ... a restlessness and a desire as yet so intangible that it was no more disturbing than the faint elusive snatch of a dream in that fleeting moment of the awakening.

She rose from her chair.

'I think I'll go in.' No edge of aggression in her voice now, nor arrogant defiance in her eyes. She felt strangely at peace; it was like the calm after great turbulence. Nigel's eyes were lazy, yet perceptive. He said, an odd inflection in his voice,

'I'm going for a stroll – I don't suppose you'd care to come with me?'

She frowned then, because of the swift affirmative reaction to his words, for she had nodded even as he spoke.

'I – I . . .'

'Yes, Liz?' A sideways, upward glance, amused and faintly mocking. 'You were about to say something?'

Did he sense her emotion? Liz swallowed, calling up her dislike of this man, her resistance, her immunity. They failed her and she found herself saying,

'Yes, I'd like a walk.'

He looked down for a brief moment, as if unwilling to reveal his expression, but she sensed his triumph and, surprisingly, was not infuriated by it. He rose, and with graceful feline ease he straightened up. How tall he was! – head and shoulders above her. And how straight and slim, muscled and sinewed, and carrying not an ounce of surplus flesh.

They strolled through the courtyard and across the grounds. A giant green lizard darted across their path and disappeared beneath a rock. From the trees the whirring sound of the cicadas filled the air. The sun was still brilliant, yet traced on the clear blue sky was the sharp outline of a crescent moon.

'Have you any preference?' Nigel spoke quietly and accommodatingly, even slackening his pace on noticing Liz's difficulty in keeping up with him. 'The village or, if you like, the Sanctuary? Or perhaps you'd merely like to go to the hotel for a drink?'

'The Sanctuary, I think.'

The Sacred Precincts in which the colossal Temple of Apollo stood were indeed the home of the gods. Through the wild primordial landscape flitted ghosts and echoes of a long-dead past, and Liz's brain reeled with the intense awareness of these haunting spirits at whose pagan altars orgiastic rites had been reverently conducted.

This hallowed site was in those ancient times considered as the navel of the earth, this being decided when Zeus, king of all the heathen gods, released two eagles, one from where the sun rose and the other from where it set, and they met at Delphi. From highest heaven Zeus lowered the *omphalos* to mark the spot. Beneath this *omphalos* lay the sacred cave of Mother Earth, from whom all life originated – or so it was believed by the pagan Greeks. The cave was guarded by the monstrous Python whom Apollo, Zeus's most loved and famous son, slew and left to rot on the side of the fearsome mountain. Above the cave was built the magnificent Temple of Apollo and for over a thousand years this sacred site, on a tiny plateau beneath the towering splendour of Parnassus, was the most hallowed place in all Greece, and the centre of culture for the whole of the known world, the cult of the Sun God Apollo being light and reason.

Nigel and Liz entered the site along the Sacred Way where once stood many small exquisitely-fashioned treasuries in which were housed the gifts offered by the numerous city states to Apollo. Magnificent statues had lined this avenue of treasuries, the most beautiful being a glittering bronze palm tree hung with golden dates and topped by a statue of Athena, also in gold.

Nigel talked of the site as they strolled along and Liz found herself enthralled as in his deep rich voice he told her of the ancient pagan rites conducted when the Pythia would inhale the vapours pouring from the chasm and which were believed to give her prophetic powers.

Of the great temple very little remained, but the ground plan was sufficient for Liz to form a picture of what it had once been like.

'It's sad that this is all that remains.' They were standing in the temple; several parties of tourists were also standing about, avidly taking in all their guides were telling them. 'Is this the original temple?'

'Indeed no. The original was made of wood and destroyed by fire; the second was destroyed by an earthquake – there have been many earthquakes here, but you probably know that.' He smiled quizzically down at her and added, 'This is not a gentle site, Liz, just the contrary, in fact . . . so it should be suited to your nature.'

She looked up, sending him a speaking glance from under her lashes. He laughed and Liz found it impossible not to respond.

'I shall become immune to your barbs, Nigel. Anything in excess becomes ineffective.'

He laughed again, probably remembering that above Apollo's Temple were written the words, 'Nothing in excess'. But all he said was,

'She has a sting too, has she? Ah, well, that can be extracted.'

'You think so? What a pompous, self-opinionated man you are!' Strange, she thought, but this banter contained no underlying animosity; on the contrary, it was surprisingly light-hearted and friendly.

'You know, Liz,' he returned, beginning to walk on again, through the temple towards the ramp at its entrance, 'you won't believe me, I know – but you're the only person who has ever called me pompous.'

'Perhaps no one else has ever had cause to do so.' He said nothing and she hesitated before adding, with a temerity which was not really intended, but the words fell from her lips even as she would have checked them, 'Some people lack the courage to say what they think.'

Strangely he took no offence, but merely flicked her a sideways glance of lazy indifference.

'By "people" I presume you're really referring to one

particular person . . . a woman?'

'Greta, yes.' Liz frowned. Somehow the very name was like sandpaper on a nerve.

'You don't like her, it would seem?' Still no apparent interest, yet Liz, with her alert mind, sensed a certain degree of eagerness in his attitude of waiting.

'I can feel nothing but contempt for a woman who gives herself to a man without marriage – or is even tempted to give herself for that matter.' They had reached the ramp and with an unconscious gesture Nigel put his hand under Liz's arm as they descended it.

'Tell me,' he said, withdrawing his hand as they reached the bottom, 'have you ever been tempted?'

'Certainly not!'

He smiled at her swift indignation and said,

'I believe you misunderstood me. What I meant was, has any man tried to tempt you?'

'The answer again is no.'

'In that case you've no proof of your own invulnerability,' he deliberated softly. 'We can all remain white if temptation never comes our way.

Somehow his pronouncement carried an odd significance and Liz looked sharply at him. His lips were curved in a half-smile, a smile of hazy recollection as if he were re-living some momentous interlude in his life. 'Even the strongest of us can succumb to temptation, Liz. Keep that in mind, always, and try to extend a little more understanding to your fellow men – and women,' he added as an afterthought. They were wandering towards the vast amphitheatre, which in ancient times was used only for religious events. Liz and Nigel began to climb the steps, which were really the seats, and they had reached the top when it was suddenly borne in on Liz that in the silence following Nigel's last words there had entered into

Liz a sense of tranquillity which she had never before experienced. Here in this abode of long-departed gods was peace, and despite the groups of camera-snapping tourists cluttering up the temple and the Sacred Way Liz became imbued with an 'aloneness' which was so satisfying and pleasant that she felt a compulsion to repeat the performance and come to the site again and again with her husband.

The sun was sinking when they left the sanctuary, and the cliffs alternated between flame and shadow before the barren peaks melted finally into a sky of purple dusk.

'Are you going out?' asked Liz as they entered the garden and the intoxicating perfume of lemon blossom reached them from the *perivoli* which occupied a sizeable area in the grounds of Nigel's house. In this orchard were also orange and mandarin trees, and walnuts and peaches.

'This evening, you mean?' Nigel glanced down at her from his great height. 'No, I'm spending it at home.'

Why should she be glad? Liz wondered . . . and would go no farther than that for, subconsciously, she shirked an answer to her question.

CHAPTER FIVE

Liz had just finished dressing when she heard the knock on her bedroom door. She frowned. Maria? But what could she want?

'Come in.' Liz was seated at her dressing-table, a perfume spray in her hand. Through the mirror she watched the door swing inwards. Nigel stood there, immaculate in a lounge suit of dark grey linen, all his innate *savoir-vivre* displayed in his poise and bearing, in the severe lines of his face, and even in the air of languid boredom with which he regarded his wife. One tawny hand rested half in and half out of his jacket pocket, the other negligently touched the jamb of the door. 'What do you want?' she demanded, swivelling round on her stool. Nigel's brows lifted slightly, but Liz received no reply as he studied her critically, absorbing every detail – from the shining glory of her hair to her daintily-clad feet. A tingle of wrath shot through her, but although she searched for some biting comment she found to her chagrin that words eluded her.

'Fine,' drawled Nigel at length.

'What do you mean – fine?'

'You'll do very well,' he responded mildly, oblivious of her swiftly-rising colour.

'You'd better explain,' she invited, endeavouring to keep her temper.

'Knowing you, I thought you might just decide to let me down.'

Anger settled; its dregs had a stimulating effect and, her face clearing, Liz actually smiled at him.

'Afraid I might appear before your guests looking something like Maria, for instance?'

'Hardly like Maria.' Nigel's voice contained its customary languor, but there was an added edge of humour to it as he continued, 'I sincerely hope that when the time comes you'll take measures to prevent your figure attaining those gargantuan proportions.'

Her blue eyes looked into his, sparklingly.

'Boredom is conducive to the putting on of weight.' With a dainty movement Liz touched the back of one ear with the nozzle of the spray.

'You couldn't resist saying that.' Nigel's green eyes flickered with amusement. 'Bored already, are you?'

'Unutterably! I'm thinking of paying a visit to England.'

His brows went up again.

'Already?'

'There was nothing in our contract to say how often I should go to England. I shall visit my home just whenever I like.'

His rather heavy lids came down, veiling his expression.

'I hope you're not forgetting you're married. You did once, remember.'

She studied him with a blank expression.

'I don't know what you mean?'

'There'll be no separation.'

Silence. Making a half turn Liz placed the perfume spray on the dressing-table.

'Are you afraid I'll leave you?'

He moved across the room, and stood beside her. Liz looked at him, neither lowering her eyes nor even blinking as she met his searching gaze.

Nigel smiled faintly to himself.

'No, I'm not afraid of that.' And at his words, spoken in so suave and confident a tone, Liz found her memory taking her back to the occasion of their visit to the Sanctuary – and to her subsequent feeling of pleasure when Nigel had declared his intention of remaining at home that evening.

It had been a pleasant, intimate sort of situation in which she had found herself. First, there had been that interlude, when in the shimmering phantom of twilight they had relaxed on the patio, awaiting the summons to dinner. The meal itself had been cosy and intimate, with Nigel ever in smiling attendance upon her. Afterwards they had strolled in the garden, in the clear crystalline air of a Grecian night. From above, an effulgence of moonlight sprinkled the towering crags of Parnassus with silver, while in the cool dark depths of the ravine impregnable shadows lurked, fearsome and grotesque. Pervading the entire landscape was the mysterious, compelling influence of Apollo's Sanctuary, with its vast temple and treasuries, lying as it did in a most dramatic setting against the sheer rock wall at the southern foot of the mighty Mount Parnassus. Liz had not only been affected by the magic unreality of the situation, she recalled, but also by some emotion she had never before experienced.

Nigel stirred at her side and she came out of her dream to glance up at him. What would he say were she to tell him of her thoughts? But why speculate on that when she had no intention of telling him of her thoughts? In fact, she was not quite sure she wanted to be civil, even, because she more than a little resented his presence in her room.

'It isn't exactly enlivening here,' she said after he had again made a small impatient move in order to draw her attention to the fact that he expected an answer to his question.

'Thanks', he returned laconically, and, when she did not speak, 'You're a thoroughly spoiled child, Liz, and I've a mind to find you some work to do — as a cure for your boredom.'

Liz stood up, an exquisitely-beautiful figure in a short dress of silver lamé, its mandarin collar stiff and high and studded with tiny seed pearls.

'I never worked before I came here and I've no intention of beginning now.'

Her husband's eyes narrowed and for a brief space it did seem that he would voice some scathing rejoinder. However, he thought better of it and, changing the subject, warned her again that he expected to have no complaints to make when the evening came to an end.

'You remember what I said?' he ended almost threateningly, and Liz's eyes became pools of blue ice.

'I said I might oblige,' she responded with a sort of acid sweetness.

'And I said you *would* oblige,' he reminded her in dangerous tones.

She frowned impatiently, but to her amazement she was still a long way from the flare-point of wrath.

'If only you wouldn't adopt this dictatorial manner with me! I wish I could find some explanation for it.'

'So I have you guessing at last?' he murmured, his voice reverting to its familiar lazy drawl. 'Keep on guessing, my dear, you might hit upon the answer in time.' And, leaving her to ponder on that obscure remark, he glanced at his watch, said he'd see her downstairs, and left the room.

You might hit upon the answer . . . ? Absently Liz gazed into the mirror, saw the lines creasing her brow and immediately stopped frowning. The answer. . . . To what?

Her vacant expression remained for a moment or two before, shrugging impatiently, Liz refused to tease herself with the matter any longer.

The dinner party went off without a hitch, and to her surprise Liz thoroughly enjoyed herself. Annette and Claire, both about Liz's age, were delighted to meet her, and surprised of course because, as Claire outspokenly declared, no one ever thought Nigel would marry an English girl.

'No one thought he would ever marry at all,' put in Annette. 'Nigel always used to say he was too fond of his freedom ever to get himself tied up permanently—' She stopped and blushed at her lack of tact. Liz merely smiled, but somehow the idea that these two girls were now thinking of Greta was like a rasp on her pride. Was it only her pride that was affected, though? Liz glanced over to where her husband was standing by the cocktail bar, deep in conversation with the three Greeks – Panos, Petrakis and Dendras. Nicoleta, Dendras's wife, was also taking part in the conversation and Liz had just learned from Claire that Nicoleta owned a fleet of cargo ships and was even more wealthy than her husband. As if sensing her interest Nigel turned his head and met his wife's gaze. The quick directness of his glance was disconcerting and she would have sought to escape by turning her attention to her companions again, but Nigel's eyes held her, making an unfathomable impact on her which, although lasting a mere few seconds, left an impression which was to remain with Liz throughout the entire evening. Presently Nigel said,

'Come on, you girls, and have a drink. Leave the feminine talk until later,' at which Annette and Claire immediately jumped up and went with Liz to join the four at the bar.

'I must congratulate you again on your marriage to so beautiful a girl,' Panos was saying as Nigel handed Liz a drink. 'How did you find her, Nigel?'

Nigel shrugged and smiled and caught Liz's half-veiled eyes.

'She was around.' He spoke in a careless tone, but Liz sensed the presence of a hidden note of satire behind his words. She could almost hear him saying, 'Yes, she's beautiful outside – but what a shrew lies underneath!' And because of this a touch of colour rose to tint her cheeks.

Some time later Nigel was saying in an undertone,

'Your blushes are enchanting.' But he just had to add, amusement playing at the corners of his eyes, 'Even when they're produced by nothing more than a guilty conscience.'

'Was there any need for that!' she flashed with a sudden stab of anger.

A smothered sound of exasperation rose in Nigel's throat.

'You're a bad-tempered wretch. I'm beginning to wonder whether I've caught you young enough,' he added, and she gave an audible gasp.

'Caught me?' He made no comment and she added, 'You might live to be sorry you caught me at all!'

'What sort of a threat is that?' he demanded, regarding her now through narrowed eyes. 'You're the most imprudent woman I've ever met.'

'The most imprudent?' she repeated tartly. 'Are you sure you don't mean the least submissive?'

Nigel quirked an eyebrow, an action that made her blood boil.

'Why the comparative? I've yet to discover even the

smallest degree of submission in you.'

Liz drew a deep breath; her mouth was tight and her eyes became militant, but whatever retort she had been about to make died on her lips, for at that moment others came within earshot.

'To be continued,' announced Nigel with a laugh, and deliberately turned away so as not to afford her the satisfaction of sending him the venomous glance which he knew she had ready.

But when the last good nights had been said and the three cars were moving slowly along the drive one behind the other, Nigel turned to Liz and in perplexing contrast to his former attitude of taunting satire he seemed almost tender as he said,

'I was proud of you, Liz – very proud indeed.'

Taken completely by surprise, Liz could only say,

'I wish I understood you, Nigel.' And, as he made no comment, 'Why did you marry me?' She watched him closely while awaiting an answer. His lids drooped, ostensibly with boredom. But Liz was fully aware that it was an evasive action, just as his voice was evasive when at length he spoke.

'Why the repeated inquiries? I've already said, marriage was the simplest way out of our difficulty.'

'The simplest, perhaps, but certainly not the most preferable. I believe you'll agree with me on that?'

'No such thing. Had not marriage been preferable to me then I should never have entered into it.' He stopped, and laughed at her expression. 'Still guessing? Well, as I remarked earlier, you might hit upon the answer in time.'

She fell silent, pondering this. Nigel had had some reason for the marriage, that went without saying. That it wasn't money was obvious because he could have obtained his inheritance by contesting the will. That it wasn't desire was equally obvious, simply because Nigel had not troubled her up till now and it was most unlikely that he ever would do so. And if neither money nor desire prompted the suggestion of marriage, then what had? How galling to be kept in the dark like this!

'I wonder what you'd have done had I refused to marry you?' she murmured presently, an odd inflection in her voice.

The three cars had disappeared, but the tail-lights of the last one were still visible through the trees. Nigel and Liz were on the patio and at her softly-spoken words her husband turned his head to look at her.

'I wonder why you didn't refuse?' he countered, side-stepping her question – at least in some small degree.

'You appear to have forgotten that I, unlike you, believed those wills to be valid.'

'So you did,' agreed Nigel with a yawn. All at once he seemed to be thoroughly bored by the conversation. 'It's time we turned in. I'm tired and I'm sure you are too.'

She nodded absently, surprising herself by accepting his deliberate digression without any attempt to redirect him on to the subject of their marriage.

'Yes . . . I am tired . . .' But although he stood aside she made no move to precede him indoors, for she was suddenly affected in some indefinable way by the soft, moon-flushed night with its thistle-down breeze wafting exotic perfumes through the air and bending the spidery palm fronds to grotesque shapes against the nebulous back-cloth of mountain cliff and crag which were themselves superimposed upon the violet and pearl of an Eastern sky.

Liz had always believed herself to be hard, appreciative of beauty while impervious to any emotional effect of it.

But who could remain immune to the subtle call of the Delphic scene? Several lines of a poem by Byron came naturally upon her thought stream and she whispered them to herself. 'Shall I unmoved behold the hallow'd scene, which others rave of though they know it not?'

The 'hallow'd scene' was intense, all-powerful in its influence, because even though by the will of the emperor Theodosius its oracular powers were long since doomed, it held on tenaciously to its glory, enfolding its god in slumber but not in death. His spirit lingered in glorious triumph, still conquering with gentle power as modern suppliants pilgrimed from the far reaches of the earth to worship in awe and wonderment at the pagan shrine. Carried away as she was by a sort of mystic enchantment, Liz even forgot her husband's presence as another swing of memory brought further lines of the poem to mind. In this '. . . wild pomp of mountain majesty . . . some gentle spirit still pervades . . . sighs in the gale, keeps silence in the cave, and glides with glassy foot o'er yon melodious wave'.

'What are you thinking about?' Soft words, and Liz turned involuntarily, a smile touching her lips.

'I was totally lost in the wonder of this place. You must be proud to have been born here.'

'One doesn't think about it very much, but – yes, I suppose I am proud to be able to say I'm a native of Delphi.'

For a moment Liz examined his face, noting the noble lines and finely-etched contours, the taut and thrusting jaw, the hard austerity of the eyes and low aristocratic forehead from which a mass of dark hair was brushed back, shining and with the merest hint of a wave.

A sudden stirring of her senses which had nothing to do with the mystery of the night or the clear heady air brought a flush to Liz's cheeks and a new and tender light to her eyes. Nigel caught his breath and before Liz had time to grasp his intention he had drawn her into his arms and his lips were seeking hers. She struggled free, but was caught again, and this time she felt his mouth on hers, warm and strong . . . and yet gentle in a way that seemed quite out of line with the disproportionate degree of mastery to which he had previously subjected her.

'Let me go!' she flared when once he had relaxed his hold. 'I told you not to try any tricks!'

'Come, Liz,' he admonished gently. 'That wasn't so very distasteful, was it?'

She glared at him, and would have twisted away, but the pressure of his hands on her arms was increased and she desisted, having no wish to acquire marks that would infuriate her for days.

'Any man's kisses would be distasteful to me. I've told you, my one fervent wish was to remain a spinster!'

'Not natural,' he drawled, releasing her and putting a small distance between them.

'Have it your own way. I'm not in the least interested in whether you consider me natural or not.' She edged past him, but turned as she reached the great glass doors leading into the salon. 'Remember what I said about not trying any tricks,' she warned softly, her eyes narrowed, yet sparkling. 'I said you'd receive a shock – and I meant it!'

To her chagrin that only produced a laugh from Nigel, and the reminder of his answer on that occasion. He had asserted that her words were suggestive of a challenge – which he was just the man to accept.

'Also, my dear,' he added, 'I have warned you, numerous times, not to try me too far. I was not wasting words when I threatened to let you have a bruise or two.'

Fury blazed from Liz's eyes, and her small fists clenched so tightly that the bones of her knuckles shone through the skin. And yet she held a curb on her tongue, astounded by the discovery that her anger stemmed more from the fact of his creating disunity than from his actual words – or even his kiss. Determined to quell her anger, she said quietly,

'Your threats are already becoming ineffective—' She managed to smile sweetly at him. 'Owing to their repetition.'

Nigel laughed and Liz's eyelids flickered. Somehow, she was impelled to hide her expression from him.

'Were my threats ever effective?' he wanted to know, cocking an eyebrow in a manner that should by rights have infuriated her.

'No, they weren't. Nor could they ever be. What I should have said,' she added with a sort of affable spite, 'is that they are beginning to bore me.'

A moment's silence followed. From the olive trees came the nocturnal whirr of the cicadas and an occasional note of music on the green-clothed foothills of Parnassus – sheep bells tinkling through the still clear air.

'Bore you, do they?' Nigel smiled faintly to himself. 'How typical of the British landed gentry! Everything bores them.'

'I never said everything bores me,' she retorted with indignation but not with anger.

'Earlier this evening you said you were bored with this place.'

Liz was shaking her head.

'I realize now that I couldn't ever be bored with this place.'

Nigel's eyes flickered oddly at the tone of her voice. It

was soft – like a caress almost, and quite alien to the irascible voice she kept especially for her husband.

'So you've changed your mind about going to England?' was all he said, but the words, which were more a statement than a question, were suggestive of a surrender on her part and this she could not accept.

'Not at all; I want to visit my home – and remain in it for a while.'

Nigel was staring ahead, to where the smiling moon hung, clear and brilliant over the dark expanse of sea.

'When are you thinking of going?' he inquired, resting his back against one of the columns supporting the verandah.

'Soon – next week, probably.' Her voice was a challenge; Nigel ran his eye over her but said equably,

'How long will you be away?'

His easy manner suggested disinterest, which was what she wanted, Liz told herself . . . but why, then, this feeling of pique?

'That's impossible to say. It depends on how many invitations I receive,' she added with a deliberate flash of defiance.

'You must have some idea how long you'll be away?'

'I've just said I haven't.' A cloud obscured the moon, and the garden was veiled in shadow, but the verandah itself was bathed in a diffusion of soft amber light provided by the lanterns hanging at intervals among the spreading canopy of vines.

Nigel contemplated Liz in silence; she noted the swift gleam of danger in his eyes; all at once his manner changed to one of arrogant implacability.

'You'll be away a fortnight, and no longer,' he murmured gently at last.

Liz's mouth tightened.

'I'll stay away just as long as I like!'

A deep sigh from her husband.

'Shall we continue the argument tomorrow?' he suggested. 'As I've remarked, we're both tired.'

The cloud sailed by, ferried by a high-altitude wind, and the moon shone brilliantly down again, immersing the entire landscape in a silver luminescence. Strangely, Liz had no difficulty in suppressing the irritation aroused by her husband's rather testily-spoken words. But of course she could not allow him to think he had won even one small point.

'Yes, Nigel, we'll continue the argument tomorrow ... and there *will be* an argument,' she added, sending him a smile – a smile that held no trace of humour.

However, the argument was not to be continued the following morning. Immediately after breakfast Nigel announced his intention of going to Athens. He would be away about a week to ten days, he said. The decision appeared to have been made suddenly, after reading his morning mail.

'If you're away ten days then I'll have left for England before you return.' She expected a repetition of last night's order that she stay away a fortnight and no longer. But he merely nodded absently and within a few minutes of leaving the breakfast table he had left the house.

Later in the day she was on the lawn, a book beside her. Her eyes were half-closed. Bored to distraction, she was mentally cursing her great-grandfather when Nikos appeared to announce Nigel's cousin. Liz's swift smile of welcome was received with unconcealed pleasure as Spiros motioned to Nikos to fetch him the chair which stood a few yards away on the terrace.

'You're acquiring a lovely tan,' he observed, slouching in the chair and resting his feet on a bar running underneath the wickerwork garden table. His attitude, which was one of sloth, brought a sudden frown to Liz's brow, but she was glad of his company and, despite this petty annoyance, she was about to open a conversation with him when he spoke again. 'Where's Nigel? I have a message for him from my mother. There's a christening coming up in the family and they want Nigel to be godfather.'

'Nigel's gone away this morning – to Athens, on business.'

'He has? He'll be back tomorrow?'

'He'll be away at least a week.'

An odd expression entered his eyes.

'Why didn't you go with him? I thought you wanted to visit Athens.'

'His time will be fully occupied with business,' she said after a small interlude during which she sought vainly for some other excuse for her not accompanying Nigel to the capital. 'I'd have been bored, walking about on my own.'

'You'd have found more to do in Athens than you'll find to do here. Are you going to stick in the garden all the time?' She made no reply and Spiros added, 'It's a funny set-up, this.'

'What do you mean?'

'Nigel . . . to go off without his wife. It's not natural, especially as you're newly-married.' Spiros shook his head, plainly puzzled by the whole situation. And because his mind was running along a particular line, plus the fact that he was completely without tact, he said, musingly, 'Greta's also in Athens . . .' And then he tailed off, realizing what he had implied.

'She is?' Liz felt a stab of anger and wondered at it. The natural thing was for her to feel satisfaction that

Nigel had gone to Greta. Thus occupied he would not be turning his attention to his wife. That was what she desired, to be ignored – at least in *that* way. 'When did she go?'

'Two or three days ago.' His face was flushed. 'I say, Liz, I'm the greatest fool in all Greece! There's no connection, believe me – there can't be!' He did not sound too sure, though, and added, as if to convince himself as much as Liz, 'Nigel's not the one to let you down, you can be sure of that. If he's gone on business then he'll keep his mind on business.'

'You don't believe that, do you?' she said, disconcerting him.

'Didn't he ask you to go with him?' Spiros deliberately side-tracked her question.

Liz shook her head absently. Nigel and Greta in Athens – and Nigel having previously said that she was not to go there with Spiros. Suddenly her fury was like a burning vapour encompassing her whole body.

'As he's going to be away,' she said with determined control, 'there's no reason why you and I shouldn't take that trip to the capital.'

Spiros's jaw dropped at her suggestion.

'Aren't you afraid of Nigel?' he blurted out.

Liz's blue eyes were hard as agate.

'I'm not afraid of anyone.'

Spiros shook his head.

'I wish I knew what this was all about. There's some mystery. Why did you two marry?'

'That,' she said brusquely, 'is our business. Are you going to take me to Athens?' This was deliberate defiance, Liz knew. And she didn't care if Nigel should see her with Spiros. In fact, she hoped he did, for he himself would be with Greta, and so he would find himself in the galling position of being unable to voice an objection.

'I'd love to take you.' Spiros's eyes became admiring and eager. 'But Nigel would kill me.'

A half sneer curved her mouth.

'Don't be melodramatic, Spiros. When shall we go?'

'It's convenient any time ... but ...' He hesitated doubtfully.

'We're cousins. You said yourself that it would be quite in order for us to go to Athens together.'

'I did say that,' he agreed, but went on to remind Liz that Nigel had forbidden them to go to Athens together.

Liz merely waited, aware that Spiros was almost ready to fall in with her suggestion. She smiled and for once felt grateful for her charms. Spiros would not be able to resist her request.

And she was right. He was as putty in her hands, and although he did retain a troubled look he said he would call for her early the following morning.

'Let's hope we don't run into Nigel,' he added, 'for if we do there'll be the very devil to pay. I hope you'll shoulder the entire blame?'

Liz only laughed. She could deal with Nigel, she thought, chiding Spiros for his fear.

He arrived at nine o'clock the following morning, his apprehension had entirely evaporated and he was intending thoroughly to enjoy the trip.

It was a four-hour journey and they arrived in Athens in time for lunch, which they took at a restaurant in Omonia Square, after having the greatest difficulty in parking their car. The crowds Liz had seen in London were nothing to what she saw here. From the window of the restaurant she watched the policeman on point duty. The traffic arrangement was like a frustrating puzzle, yet

Liz knew there was some system – some quite amazing system – and yet cars, buses, scooters and a dozen other assorted vehicles whizzed from every corner and merged – miraculously without one huge pile-up – and then whizzed off again in their respective directions. Pedestrians stood, literally by their thousands, one eye on the little green man and the other on the policeman, who every minute or so, would blow a piercing blast on his whistle. When all traffic had come to a halt solid blocks of humanity would surge forward, like opposing armies bent on a head-on collision.

Later, from the balcony of her hotel room high above the square she stood, fascinated, and watched the mêlée again crossing the roads. Where were they all going, these scurrying little ants with their brown, determined faces?

'I've never ever seen such crowds,' she said to Spiros later when, on entering the hotel lounge, she joined him. 'It's obviously going to be like this all the time. One won't be able to move!'

'We're in the busiest part of the city,' Spiros reminded her. 'No, it won't be like this all the time.'

It was now early evening and, leaving the car on the hotel park, they wandered out into the city.

They made for the Plaka, through a hodgepodge of alleyways and streets with their *tavernas* and clubs from which emanated the pungent odour of burning flesh – kebabs cooking on the charcoal stoves. *Bouzouki* strains mingled with the rising crescendo of laughter and chatter and music from a discotheque. Through the open doors Liz caught sight of male dancers, leaping through the intricate performance of the *syrtaki,* or the more sober *tsamiko.*

The lights and noise, the men sprawled at pavement

tables playing cards, the flower-sellers pushing their blooms at every tourist, the doormen at the clubs inviting entry . . . all this contrasted in modern abandon with the tranquil scene above, where softly-coloured lights moved imperceptibly to illuminate first one building and then another on the Acropolis, standing in high regal splendour and disdain above the mad whirl and disorder of the Plaka, the old part of the city which, because it carried all the charm of the East, was now being geared to tourism.

'What a pity,' breathed Liz as they slid on to the road to avoid an insistent woman trying to pin flowers on their clothes. Already many people looked like something out of a carnival. 'It must have been marvellous once.'

'It still is. The atmosphere during the day is totally different. We'll come along in the morning if you like.'

She nodded, thoroughly enjoying the new experiences despite her remark. Her eyes went again to the lights above – mauve and blue and a soft golden yellow. The set immobile faces of the caryatids seemed to frown on the frivolity down below.

'We'll find somewhere to eat,' suggested Spiros. 'Do you want to stay round here?'

'Yes, I think so.'

Spiros knew just the place. Its entrance was unpretentious, but once inside Liz had all the atmosphere she could have desired. A vine-covered trellis formed the roof which was criss-crossed with strings of coloured lights. On a dais dancers in native costume were performing the lively *kalamatianos* to the haunting strains of the *bouzouki* band, while the diners chattered and consumed enormous amounts of Greek food and wine.

'Have you enjoyed it?' Spiros asked on their way up in the lift.

'It was wonderful, and exciting,' she responded enthusiastically, and it wasn't until she was in her bedroom that she realized that her first day in Athens had not been quite perfect. Why? Spiros was good company; he was witty and pleasant and fairly good-looking. Yet something had been missing, something vital. Opening the window, Liz stepped out on to the balcony; traffic continued to surge through the square and it seemed that one could not put a pin between the lights.

Liz's thoughts went automatically to her husband – who was somewhere in this city with his girl-friend. Obviously Greta was not troubled by the conventions and strict customs forbidding a Greek woman to consort with a man before marriage. Still musing, and staring with unseeing eyes down to the conglomeration of humanity and traffic below, Liz found herself admitting that, if Nigel had tempted Greta – and of course he must have done – then the Greek girl would have had to be exceedingly strong to resist him. Following on this came the recollection of Nigel's assertion that all could remain white if temptation never came their way. He had gone on to remark that even the strongest could succumb to temptation . . . The words had registered, true, and fairly strongly, but only now did Liz stop to analyse them – or, rather, endeavour to analyse them. Even the strongest of us . . . Those were his exact words, and he had been caught up in reflection, she recalled. It was just as if he himself had been tempted . . . and had succumbed. Did that mean he hadn't really wanted to have an affair with Greta, but had been unable to resist her charms? It would seem so, and as Liz dwelt on this she suddenly became conscious of a strange uncomprehensible sensation of optimism, and frowned at the idea.

Why should such a feeling enter into her? It reminded

her of her childhood, and her excitement as a birthday drew near. But this present feeling? It was not even tangible. Let alone explicable. Restless, and for the first time in her life, bewildered, she turned at last and closed the windows, then the shutters, and the noise was considerably deadened. The big air-conditioned room was cool and fresh after the sultry night air outside and despite her teasing bewilderment of mind she fell into a restful, dreamless sleep.

They had resolved to spend four days in the city and after an exhausting three days' sight-seeing they decided to spend the last day in a more restful manner. Soon after breakfast they drove to Cape Sounion where, after lunching at the Tourists' Restaurant, they found an uncrowded beach and spent the entire afternoon between swimming in the warm sea and sunbathing on the sands.

The following morning they set out early for home, and although Liz had previously told herself that an encounter with Nigel would not have troubled her in the least, she found herself feeling immeasurably thankful that such an encounter had not taken place.

CHAPTER SIX

ALTHOUGH she enjoyed the trip Liz had experienced an unaccountable void and a subsequent feeling of unrest which detracted from a full appreciation of all she had seen. Unaccountable ...? Why try to disguise the truth? There was no one to deceive but herself, so she might as well confess that she would far rather have had her husband's company than that of his cousin. A wry smile fluttered at the admission; had she and Nigel gone on that trip together the result would have been a prolonged slanging match from the moment they left home until they returned. It was strange, but she had never before contemplated a friendship with Nigel; he represented the male arrogance which in all other men she had known had struck her as pathetic because of the struggle they had to maintain it. She felt nothing but contempt for their struggles and failing pomposity; their weaknesses disgusted her.

And that was one reason why she had never contemplated marriage. But she was forced to acknowledge the strength of her husband, in whom the very idea of weakness would be laughable, and in this compulsive moment of honesty Liz decided she would not be averse to entering into a friendship with her husband. Such an occurrence must inevitably require a burying of animosity on both their parts, she mused, and then accepted the fact that she was the only one to bear animosity. Nigel's great fault was that maddening attitude of mocking satire he adopted towards her, which he very well knew brought out the worst in her.

'You're very quiet?' Spiro's voice at her side jerked Liz from her meditations and she turned her head. Having left Athens well behind, they were now driving through the Plain of Thebes, entering Dionysos country where in those pagan times long since dead the handsome young god would sport shamelessly with the nymphs of Mount Helikon.

'I'm enjoying the scenery.' She had no wish to open a conversation with Spiros and even though she had a twinge of conscience over this she fell silent again, desiring nothing more than to be left to appreciate her surroundings.

The barren slopes of Mount Kithaeron looked stark and gruesome and Liz found herself drifting off into a contemplation of the scene when the infant Oedipus, his feet riveted together, had been abandoned on these fearsome rocks by his father, Laius, because an oracle had prophesied that when Oedipus grew up he would commit patricide. But the baby was found by a shepherd and named Oedipus because of his swollen feet. Later, Oedipus was told by the Delphic Oracle that he would murder his father and marry Jocasta, Laius's wife, who was Oedipus's own mother. The prophecy was of course to come true. Other dark deeds had been perpetrated hereabouts, as for example the orgiastic rites indulged in by women on the magpie-haunted moors below the mountain. These women would tear animals to pieces and devour their flesh. On one occasion Agave and her nymphs, in their wild frenzy, mistook Agave's son for a wild beast. After he was dismembered and parts of his body devoured, Agave held up his head, blood running from her mouth and down her breasts. It was only when Cadmus, her aged father, spoke to her that she realized what she had done. Distracted by grief, she began to fondle the head and to voice the beautiful lament:

'. . . Alas, no more my son . . . O gracious form, that wondering men beheld . . . O haughty brows before which Thebes bowed . . . Torn, rent asunder, scattered, cast abroad.'

'You're miles away.' Spiros spoke again, taking his eyes off the road for a second to slant her a smiling glance.

'And ages,' she laughed. 'I was thinking of such people as Oedipus and Agave and her ill-fated son Pentheus.'

'Pentheus? Some say he was her husband.'

'So I've heard, but the lament definitely refers to Pentheus as her son. In any case, it was an unbelievably horrid murder.'

'It's all unbelievable,' laughed Spiros. 'You're in the realms of mythology, remember.'

'Quite literally,' she returned, glancing through the window again. The Helikon range, haunt of the Muses, ran from east to west, its slopes a miracle of colour as the sun began to slant, giving birth to the shades of approaching dusk – luminous mauves and pearls and brilliant crimson and gold. A spread of pink satin cloud dropped gently over the mountain summit – enfolding the gods in sleep, Liz thought, smiling at her fanciful picture-making.

Parnassus country now, with the wild savage mountain summits melting into a flame-licked sky.

The wild country . . . How it suited her! Liz's spirit was kin to the untamed massif which, through turbulence and upheaval had been born – long, long ago, before its idol-worshipping peoples had evolved even beyond the stage of the single-celled protozoa from which they came into being. So many eons without man . . . Would it see the extinction of man, and still raise its savage head to the primeval sky?

Darkness fell, swift as a curtain, and on a lonely stretch of road the car engine began to give trouble, then stopped altogether.

'What the dickens is wrong with it?' Apologetic but also bad-tempered, Spiros got out and lifted the bonnet. 'Can you shine the torch? You'll find it on the shelf under the dash.'

A quarter of an hour went by before another car drew into the side of the road and stopped, the driver offering his assistance.

Spiros had no idea what was wrong and neither had the other man.

'Can I give you a tow?' he offered at last, and thankfully Spiros accepted. The other driver was going to Arachova; here Spiros found a mechanic who, after several hours, managed to get the car moving. It limped into Delphi at five minutes to midnight. Much earlier Liz had rung to tell Nikos she would be home and there was one solitary light at the front of the house.

The Greek servant appeared immediately the car stopped; after handing out Liz's luggage Spiros was off again, anxious to reach his own home without further mishap.

Nikos had switched on the outside lights. He looked at her rather woodenly, she thought, but she was too exhausted by the prolonged journey to take much notice.

On reaching the bedroom door Nikos made an almost imperceptible hesitation – as if to add just the right amount of drama to the situation before, with what could only be described as a flourish, he swung the door inwards. Liz stepped over the threshold, then stopped, to stare disbelievingly at the bed. Her eyes flickered towards Nikos; at the deepening of her colour his face became a sniggering mask. She had an almost irrepressible urge to slap him across his face.

'You may go!'

'Yes, Mrs. Nigel.' He put her suitcases down; viciously she kicked the door even before Nikos was through it and he jumped as it hit his back.

Inflamed, Liz spoke aloud; what she said was unprintable. She stood quite still, in the silence following the slamming of the door, her face fused with crimson, the result, partly, of the humiliation she had just suffered. Her fury could have led to murder, had her husband been here. Where was he? Many questions flitted vaguely through a brain rendered almost useless by the blind fury in which it was enveloped. A double bed ... no need for questions there; its presence spoke for itself. Nigel ... Why had he cut short his visit to Athens? And how long had he been home? Greta ... Where did she fit into this new scheme of things? – or rather, the scheme of things Nigel was planning. Some hopes! So often Liz had searched for a reason for the marriage. He had her guessing; she might eventually hit upon the reason why he had married her. Well, it would appear to have been desire, after all, that had prompted him to marry her, and yet ... Something puzzling. Why should he have waited until now?

Suddenly Liz's nerves tensed; she spun round as the door opened. Nigel entered, clad in a black and gold dressing-gown, his hair tousled. Obviously he had been to bed. The door closed with an ominous click and Liz's heart jerked, then began to pound unevenly. Nevertheless, her anger bore her aloft over any intruding fear and her eyes were sparks ready to set off a conflagration as a burning vapour of fury suffused her whole quivering body.

'What's the idea! Is this some sort of a joke? Nikos – standing there sniggering at me! How dare you humiliate me before a servant!' Nigel merely leant against the door, his face a study of indolent calm. 'What is this all about?' she spat out, maddened by his composure.

He remained by the door, regarding her lazily through half-closed eyes. He began to yawn and lifted a slender brown hand to his mouth, his glance moving to her fists, clenched tight with anger, and then to the bed, exchanged only that afternoon for the single one which was now in his own room. Watching him, Liz felt her fury must surely suffocate her. And to think that only a short while ago she had decided to be more amicable, so that she and Nigel would have a chance of becoming friends. She must have been out of her mind!

'Don't be naïve,' he drawled, totally unaffected by her furious outburst. 'Once again my warnings have fallen on deaf ears, so now comes the reckoning.'

Her eyes kindled with perception.

'You know I've been to Athens with Spiros?' Defiant, her attitude as the question was phrased – but she swallowed convulsively for all that, because of the feeling of doom that was slowly creeping over her.

'I know you've been to Athens with my cousin.' Soft words, almost amicable in fact, but Liz was not lulled into a sense of security. The white drifts of rage at the sides of his mouth, the flexed jaw beneath which a nerve pulsated, out of control; these spelled danger and despite her own white-hot fury she practised caution, controlling her voice as she said,

'You saw me?'

'You were seen by Dendras.'

'Dendras?' Liz paled. Such a possibility as that of being seen by one of Nigel's friends had never for one moment entered her head. 'Where d-did he s-see us?' Automatically she stepped back, aware that Nigel now experienced difficulty in curbing his temper.

'Going up to your room in the hotel—'

'Room? Rooms, if you please! And if your friend made the implication that Spiros and I – that we ...' She stopped, then added, fire in her eyes, 'I'll deal with him! How dare he pry and carry tales!' Caution was not long in being swamped as Liz became seized by a feeling of injustice. 'Did he happen to know why you were in Athens? Did he know you had gone there to be with your pillow friend?'

'My—?' A small movement in Nigel's throat, as if he were trying to rid himself of some blockage. 'You're expand on that accusation!' At the guttural flick of his voice, ominous and vibrating, she lost a little more of her colour.

'Greta.' Liz glanced away from him, hoping she did not look as white as she felt. 'You were with her.'

'Was I? How did you reach that conclusion?'

Liz was at a loss. She had nothing at all on which to go – except her own swiftly-reached conclusion, which she now realized could be all wrong. It was owing to this conclusion that she had decided to defy her husband and go away with Spiros.

'She was in Athens, so it's logical that you were together. You made up your mind quite suddenly.'

'Who told you Greta was in Athens?'

'Spiros.'

'I see. Well, for your information I was not with Greta. I went to Athens on business and returned only because of what I heard from Dendras. I phoned Nikos to find out when you'd be back.' His eye flickered to the silver clock on her dressing-table. 'I remained up until eleven.' His tone decreased in volume until, on the last word, it was barely more than a whisper – or a snarl, she thought, a low animal sound portending danger. Liz moistened her lips.

'I thought you would be with Greta,' she said, fear rising, fear that only served to increase her anger. Why should she be afraid of this man?

'So your defiance was an act of revenge?' Soft tones still, but his expression was strange. He looked for something, searched her very soul, or so it seemed to Liz. She suddenly wished she had a better understanding of his character. What was he looking for? What were his thoughts?

'Yes,' she admitted in an unsteady voice, 'it was an act of revenge.'

He took a step towards her and again she stepped back. The action seemed to release the coiled spring of his fury, for suddenly his eyes blazed. He moved again and Liz was trapped in a grip of iron. She tried to wrench her shoulders away, but those evil fingers savaged her soft white flesh and she caught her lower lip between her teeth to stifle her rising cry of pain.

'Spiros – what do you mean by going away with him! And to be seen in the hotel – by my friend! My friend—!' All control fled and Liz felt herself caught in a cyclone; her hair smothered her face as, Nigel's temper climaxing to a crescendo of unbridled rage, she was shaken, for the second time, until the blood pounded in her head. 'To subject me to such humiliation! By God, girl, you're asking for something you'll remember for the rest of your life! How did you persuade Spiros to disregard my orders—?' He shook her again. 'How? Answer me!'

Trembling from head to foot, Liz could only regard him in wordless silence for a long moment, managing to speak only when it seemed he would subject her to more of his violence.

'I – I was bored, and – and asked Spiros to take me. I never expected to be seen by anyone who knew you.'

'I'll bet you didn't! And me — weren't you afraid of running into me?' Liz felt the pressure increase on her arms and winced, though inwardly. She was loath to let Nigel know just how much he was hurting her.

'The possibility did occur to me, but as I thought you'd be with Greta . . .' She tailed off, further explanation being unnecessary.

'So you believed that if you did see me I shouldn't be able to complain?' His voice had lost its burr of wrath, but his eyes still held their smouldering heat. 'I'm not pretending that *your* attitude surprises me, but Spiros — I'm amazed that *he* wasn't afraid of my seeing you together.'

Spiros had been afraid, but Liz could not see any gain in mentioning that just now, and although she knew Nigel was waiting she merely shook her head. In spite of her innate strength she was fully spent, both mentally and physically, and to her chagrin tears started to her eyes. Nigel was tired too and he lifted a hand to stifle a yawn; Liz believed he was going to strike her — although when she thought about it afterwards she could not understand why she should have done so — and with swiftly-renewed fury she fetched him a vicious slap across his wrist. The slap had no effect on Nigel other than to produce a look of surprise; its effect on Liz was a badly broken nail, which she had caught on the wide gold bracelet of Nigel's wrist watch. She stared at it in dismay. It was broken down to the quick.

Knocking his other hand off her arm, she snatched up a pair of scissors from the dressing-table and began cutting away the broken nail.

'What was that for?' His temper had practically subsided, a hint of humour replacing the fury in his voice.

'I thought you were going to strike me,' she snapped,

continuing to cut at the nail and realizing it would be months before it was perfect again.

'You did? And that was your reaction?'

'Hit me and you can be very sure I'll hit you back!'

Heavy lids fell over the grey-green eyes. It was a half lazy, half bored mannerism and Liz could have struck out at him again.

'Sounds like a thrown gauntlet,' murmured Nigel, with a return of his indolent drawl.

Her teeth snapped, and in one impulsive moment she threw the scissors at him. They were small and blunt-ended, so could not have done any damage had they reached their mark. However, Nigel dodged out of the line of fire and they dropped on to the carpet. For a moment he stared at them, then his eyes moved upwards, to Liz.

'Pick them up,' he ordered softly.

Her brows lifted, and so did her chin.

'Pick them up yourself!' She turned away, but through the long wall mirror saw him move purposefully towards the dressing-table. He picked up a hairbrush and she shot round to face him, her face and neck flooding with colour.

'You dare—'

'Are you going to pick them up?' An unmistakable threat in his voice and gaze. Liz's lashes fluttered down. Fury and defiance fought with caution – and fear. 'I once warned you I'd inflict a few bruises,' he murmured, regarding her in some amusement. 'I assure you, Liz, that unless you obey me you're not going to enjoy the next few minutes – although I'm quite sure I shall,' he added with a laugh. 'Well ...?' he challenged as the undecided moments passed.

Wordlessly Liz picked up the scissors and placed them

on the dressing-table.

'I detest you,' she hissed, facing him. 'I wish with all my heart I'd never married you.' She was still hot, both from anger and from humiliation at having meekly to obey his order. 'Don't be too confident, Nigel,' she advised as the humour lines at the corners of his eyes fanned out. 'I promised I'd keep to my bargain and never leave you . . . but I'm quite capable of changing my mind.'

Had he given a little start? she wondered. Could she hold the threat over his head and force him to drop the idea he undoubtedly had of staying here tonight?

After a searching scrutiny of her flushed features Nigel smilingly shook his head.

'You're a minx and a vixen, Liz, but you're also trustworthy. I believe your word is your bond and it would surprise me – no, shock me – were I to discover I was wrong in my reading of your character.'

Against her will she was impressed by his trust in her integrity. But it gave her no satisfaction, simply because, by this implicit trust, any threat she had in mind was rendered worthless. She maintained a silence and with a gesture of sardonic amusement Nigel glanced at the bed.

'Obviously you don't approve of the switching round of the – er – furniture. I had it done immediately on my return – after having learned of your escapade. I had no intention of allowing you to go off to England unpunished.' With a sort of amused deliberation he returned the hairbrush to the dressing-table. 'Given time I might have lost the desire to punish you . . .' He tailed off, laughing at her as, influenced by some compulsion, she glanced at the bed. 'You've asked for it, Liz, deliberately goading me even though my repeated warnings must surely have convinced you that my patience is far from inexhaustible.' His voice was almost apologetic, like that of a reluctant but well-meaning parent about to chastise a child. 'You have a lesson to learn,' he went on evenly. 'It's taking you a long time, but you'll learn it in the end, I assure you of that.'

Her eyes had begun to blaze as he spoke, but she turned away and stood by the open window, vaguely aware of the familiar background noises of cicadas trilling their nocturnal chant into the scented air, of sheep bells tinkling on the hillsides and the mournful hoot of an owl. From some lonely square of infecund earth drifted the protesting cry of a tethered donkey. How cruel the Greeks were to their animals; dogs, cats, goats, sheep ... none were considered to possess feelings.

She turned and examined her husband's face. Not cruelty, exactly, but ruthlessness and arrogance. The inborn air of superiority characterizing the pagans from whom he sprang.

'What does Dendras ... think?' She spoke softly, a strange hurt in her voice.

'What do you expect him to think?'

Even as indignation began to flash in her eyes she became aware of the relative indifference in his tone.

'I don't believe he thought that.'

Surprisingly Nigel smiled and his expression changed to one of amusement.

'What does "that" mean?'

Her lashes dropped, sending adorable shadows on to her cheeks.

'You know what I mean.' And after a slight pause, 'He didn't, did he?'

A faint sigh of anger and she wished she had not broached the subject. For some unknown reason she recalled her earlier admission that she would have preferred

Nigel's company to that of Spiros.

'He would have thought plenty had I not informed him that the visit had been made with my consent and approval.'

Her eyes opened.

'You said that?'

'Was there any other way I could avoid ridicule?' Abrupt now, his tones, and censorious.

'You . . . What did – what do you think?'

He regarded her in silence for a space and then, curiously,

'Is that important to you?'

She nodded without hesitation.

'Yes – strangely, it is.'

A low incredulous laugh echoed through the room.

'Then, my dear, there's hope for – for you.'

She frowned, searching his face. Why the hesitation? What had he really been about to say?

'You haven't answered my question.'

'I've already said I trust you.'

'Thank you.' The words came with difficulty, for it cost her a great deal to utter them. 'And you weren't with Greta? That's the truth?'

Again he laughed.

'You appear to be quite disproportionately troubled about my relationship with Greta.'

She wanted to deny this, but with honesty could not, so she evaded an answer by saying,

'Are you quite serious about – about staying here to-night?'

'Quite serious.' The very economy of words was significant of inflexibility. Liz gave a deep and shuddering sigh.

'It seems, then, that *you* are not to be trusted to keep

your word.'

'Is that a challenge?'

'Certainly it's a challenge. We both made promises. I've kept mine so I expect you to keep yours.'

'Then you're in for a disappointment. You shall pay for flaunting my wishes.'

Temper flared again; she turned her back on him.

'I should have known that you weren't to be trusted. Men are all the same; they've no regard for the feelings of others. That's why I intended never to marry.'

No comment. A movement at her back; arms embracing – those bands of steel whose strength she had first known that day at the fair. There had been no escaping them then ... and there was no escaping them now. She had plenty of fight within her, that was true, and with any other man she would have stood a chance, but Nigel ... Pretence was not only useless but cowardly; she must face up to the inevitable, galling as was the acceptance of defeat. She was trembling and he discovered this, for he held her very close, his chin against her cheek. She heard his breathing; the passion of anger had given way to the even stronger passion of desire.

'Afraid, are you?' He kissed her neck, then turned her round to face him. Her last faint remnant of hope died as she saw the expression in his eyes, and yet she tried to twist away. His reaction was to hold her even more firmly, while his lips crushed hers possessively, and with an ardour that made her wonder what sort of blood he had in his veins. Wild pagan blood from the ancient Hellenes – flaunters of all convention, untamed transgressors on the chastity of women.

Instinctively she put soothing fingers to her mouth when at last he relaxed his hold and held her from him, his features the carved mask of the conqueror.

'We've wasted enough time, my lovely wife.' He released her. 'Would you attempt to run away, I wonder?' Smiling, he produced a key from his pocket. 'Savours of the melodrama, I fear, but although I trust you under ordinary circumstances . . .' He smiled quizzically at her. 'These are not ordinary circumstances, are they?' She stood there, tight-lipped, and he continued, still amused by the situation, 'They could be ordinary circumstances if both of us were willing, but as I'm about to force my attentions upon you—'

'Get out!' she couldn't help interrupting, even though she knew it would avail her nothing. He meant to leave while she undressed, apparently, but there was not a shadow of doubt that he would return.

'Have a care, Liz,' he cautioned. 'Were my temper to be aroused again you could have a most unpleasant time before you.'

She did not doubt it as, pale now and resigned, she looked into his face. She had only herself to blame. She should never have married him, disliking him so intensely as she did.

'If you mean to go, then do so, but please be quiet when you lock the door. Unless I'm very much mistaken that busybody of a Greek servant of yours will have his ears alert, for I'm sure he's extremely interested in what might transpire.'

Her quiet acceptance of the situation brought a sudden curious gleam to her husband's eyes, an expression half wondering, half puzzled. Absently he tossed up the key, caught it, then regarded it thoughtfully as it lay in the palm of his hand.

'Perhaps there's no call for the melodrama, after all . . . Is there, Liz . . .?'

She threw him a savage glance; her mouth was still

tight, her eyes glittering with frustration and rage.

'I'll not come to you willingly, if that's what your pompous, arrogant mind has decided! You'll fight for what you take ... and I hope the result will be wormwood in your mouth!'

With mocking satire his gaze rested on her clenched fists.

'Wormwood, do you say?' His eyes moved to her face. He shook his head. 'No, my lovely Liz, not wormwood ... but ambrosia!'

CHAPTER SEVEN

GREAT-GRAN sat knitting as usual; Aunt Rose was by the fire, reading contentedly, while Uncle Oliver, seated at the other side of the fireplace, was playing a game of chess all by himself.

'Your move,' he would mutter now and then, and Liz would look up from her magazine and frown with irritation.

'You can't play that game alone,' she said at last. 'Why don't you play patience?'

'Because I like chess. Now . . . if I move my bishop there . . . he'll have to protect his king, so he'll place his rook there—'

'Why should he? What's wrong with his taking your bishop with this knight?' Leaning over, Liz tapped it with her finger.

'Liz,' said her uncle testily, 'do leave the game to me. I know exactly what I'm doing.'

'He always wants to win,' submitted Aunt Rose, diverted from her book. 'He cheats all the time, making the other player do all sorts of silly things.'

Liz sighed. Old age. Her glance travelled to Great-Gran. Through the old lady's sparse white hair her scalp shone, pink and clean. Her cheeks were sunken right in because Great-Gran could not abide her false teeth. Her bony hands were active now but the doctor had only yesterday predicted they would be stiffened very soon by the swiftly-encroaching rheumatism. The doctor had been brought in by Liz because Great-Gran had had a fall — only from her chair on to the thick carpet, but her breathing had been so badly affected that Liz had become afraid.

'Heart,' the doctor had declared briefly, and then added, 'Only to be expected. Worn out; it's done very well for her up till now.'

At his words a depression had fallen on Liz, and remained with her ever since. She wondered if it were good to be with old people like this, and felt relieved that her sister was married and living away from the Hall. A faint smile touched Liz's lips at the recollection of the scene when she had endeavoured to make Vivien marry Arthur. She, Liz, had been all-powerful until that unbelievable defeat which, strangely, no longer rankled. 'I'm different,' she thought, admitting – though with some reluctance – that the reason for the change was her marriage to Nigel.

She picked up her book again, but could not read, and she glanced at the clock. She was dining with Grace and her parents, but it was much too early to begin getting ready. Nevertheless, Liz could not sit still any longer and she left the room and wandered off into the grounds. Stately grounds, they were, like the house, designed at the time of the Renaissance by one of England's leading landscape gardeners of the time. No formality, just shady walks and arbours, a lake sheltered by willows, a fountain here and there and a shrubbery containing almost every type of tree that would flourish in England.

It was the end of September and the leaves were turning; this was the time of the year which Liz had loved, but now she found herself comparing her surroundings with that of her new home in Greece. She smiled faintly. One did not endeavour to compare the incomparable, the superlative. Delphi was a place apart, surpassing any other sacred shrine in the whole of Greece. Its wild mountain scenery and spuming springs, its gaping ravine and sheer rock walls; its dizzy heights where eagles planed ... these were the backcloth for the Sanctuary of Apollo – and also for her husband's home. Wandering over to a rustic garden seat, Liz sat down. It was just a week since ... A flush tipped the lovely contours of her cheeks and she actually glanced around, as if fearing someone might be near – and read her thoughts. Nigel's lovemaking had been a revelation in tenderness and gentle persuasion. He had not meant her to awake the following morning hating him. Yet the triumph had been hers – achieved through obstinacy, though. Certainly not because of revulsion. The admission lent further colour to her cheeks. Had Nigel guessed just how close she had come to surrender? She hoped he had not. If the loathing she had managed to assume the following day had anything to do with it he most certainly had not guessed. The scourge of her tongue, if as effective as she hoped, must have stripped him of any confidence he had in himself as a lover. Despite this, and the subsequent prolonged and frigid silence to which she had subjected him, she had feared he might raise an objection to her going home. But he offered none, and in fact he actually arranged her flight for her – just as if he were glad to see the back of her for a while. Paradoxically, she was piqued by this, her thoughts becoming occupied with the nagging conviction that for the next fortnight he would be enjoying himself ... with Greta. Strange it was that only a short while ago her attitude to the Greek girl was one of gratitude. She would keep Nigel from turning his attention to his wife.

Impatient with the confusion of her mind, Liz rose again and went back to the house.

'Tea's coming in a moment.' Aunt Rose produced a

smile as Liz entered the room. 'Weren't you cold out there?'

'It's not cold.'

'After Greece, it must be.'

Liz took possession of an armchair. What was the matter with her? She didn't know what she wanted. Her one desire had been to come home; now she was home she could not rest. If it weren't for the possibility of Nigel's jumping to conclusions she felt she could willingly have curtailed her visit. But with his pomposity, plus his insatiable urge to rile her, he could very well indulge in a spate of mocking comments about her not finding life with her people as interesting as it was with him. An audible, exasperated utterance broke from her lips. Even when she did return what was there to look forward to? Arguments with Nigel, or boredom in his absence.

'I wish I'd never set eyes on the man!'

'What did you say, dear?' The mild inquiry from Aunt Rose merely served to increase her impatience.

'I was talking to myself.'

'What?' Great-Gran dropped her knitting on to her knees. 'You're cold? Well, dear, that's only to be expected, seeing that you've been living in a warm country. Put a jacket on – here, do you want my shawl?'

'No, thanks, Gran,' shouted Liz, sighing.

'She didn't complain of the cold,' obliged Aunt Rose, leaning towards the old lady. 'She was talking to herself.'

The purple lobe came forward.

'What shelf?'

Liz closed her eyes. 'I can't stand it,' she thought, while wondering how she had stood it before.

'Talking to herself,' repeated Aunt Rose, her eyes brightening as the door opened and a prim maid entered with the tea tray. 'Crumpets, Maisie?'

'Yes, madam, crumpets.'

This enlivening interchange had been repeated five times since Liz's arrival last Friday. Liz waited for her uncle to speak.

'I hope you've toasted mine, Maisie?'

'Yes, sir, I've toasted yours.' With a glance at Liz Maisie proceeded to set out the tea things on a table in front of the fire. 'I've made you some sandwiches,' she smiled, and Liz thanked her.

When tea was over Liz made a speedy escape. But by the time she was dressed and in her chauffeur-driven car her dejection had cleared appreciably and she was almost her old cheerful self when, at half-past seven, she was enthusiastically greeted by her friend.

'We have half an hour before dinner,' said Grace, asking Liz to come up to her bedroom. 'I'm not quite ready, so we can talk while I dab a bit of rouge on my face and finish my manicure.' The two girls had corresponded regularly since Liz's marriage, but apart from comprehensive and flowing descriptions of Delphi and its surroundings Liz had told her friend little else, and Grace was very much in the dark concerning her private life.

'Tell me about that – about your husband. Is the arrangement working out all right?' Grace closed the bedroom door after entering in Liz's wake. 'Was it worth it – marrying for that reason, I mean?'

'To save my house and fortune?' Liz grimaced and sat down on the bed. 'To be quite honest, Grace, I don't know whether I've done right or not—' She shook her head. 'I had to think of the others, though, especially Great-Gran.'

'Never imagined you in the sacrificial role,' Grace laughed, although her gaze was serious. 'Isn't it going to work?'

'The marriage, as such, wasn't intended to work,' Liz reminded her. 'It was purely a marriage of convenience.'

Grace sat down at her dressing-table, looking at Liz through the mirror. She said curiously,

'What's he like? I know I was at the wedding, yet whenever I form a mental picture of him it's as he was at the fair — looking superior and arrogant and speaking with that affected lazy drawl.'

'The drawl's natural; it's not an affectation.' The words shot out, propelled by some unfathomable pressure which left Liz herself amazed. She hated that lazy drawl — hated it! — so why make excuses for it?

Grace's mouth rounded as she blew a soft incredulous whistle.

'You haven't fallen in love with him!' she exclaimed, staring.

'In ... love? Don't talk ridiculous, Grace!' But what was this sudden quickening of an emotion? — this faint stirring of her senses resulting from the utterance of her friend's question? It was by no means her first experience of this sensation, Liz recalled.

'No—' Grace was shaking her head. 'Not you; not the way you've always despised men, swearing you'd never marry because you'd seen through them from the moment you'd reached the age of discernment.' Grace shook her head again. 'In any case, you couldn't possibly fall in love with a man like Nigel. He's too cold and unemotional — the dispassionate type.'

Unemotional! If only Grace knew what a decidedly errant statement that was! — and it was not of her husband's unpredictable temper that Liz was thinking. Fluttering lashes hid her expression from her friend as Liz was carried back to that night, with its all-revealing interlude of Nigel's emotional make-up. Not an instant's lack of finesse, not one moment of lost control ... these seemed totally at variance with the ardency of his lovemaking. It must be experience – and of course the Greek's innate gift for the art. That Nigel was the perfect lover Liz would not deny, even though she lacked the means of comparison.

'Why the blushes?' Her friend's voice, though quiet and smooth, had the effect of making Liz jump, so completely lost was she in her thoughts.

'I'm n-not – I mean, I didn't know I was blushing.'

'Well, you are,' returned Grace, adding bluntly, 'There must be some reason for it.' No comment from Liz. Grace said strangely, 'Can I be mistaken? Can it be that the hardened confirmed spinster has fallen for the magnificent Greek – or half-Greek?' she corrected.

'I've just said no,' frowned Liz crossly.

'You haven't said any such thing. You merely told me not to be ridiculous – which could have been an attempt at evasion.'

'What would I want to fall in love with a man like that for?' snapped Liz, angry with herself for not being more cautious. Grace was no fool. In fact, she was highly intelligent, and perceptive.

'If you were in love with him it would be a far more bearable situation. The prospect of spending the rest of your life with someone you don't love can't be very pleasant.'

'I knew that when I married him.'

Grace twisted round to pick up a nail file.

'Tell me about him,' she urged. 'Is *he* quite satisfied with his bargain?'

'I expect so.' Evasion again, and this was perfectly apparent to her friend.

'What do you both do with your time?' A slight pause and then, 'Doesn't he mind living the life of a celibate?'

Liz lowered her eyes, her mind straying again to that night, and she wondered if Greta had yet learned from her maid that the beds had been changed around. No doubt of it; the sniggering Nikos would by now have passed on the news to his sister who would surely have mentioned the matter to her mistress.

'He has a pillow friend,' Liz informed Grace, who gave a little start at the expression.

'But how delicate! Is that what they call them over there?'

Absently Liz nodded, still keeping her head averted.

'Her name's Greta; they've been carrying on for ages.'

'And still are?'

Liz pondered on this. Nigel had not been with Greta in Athens, he said, and, strangely, she believed him.

'I don't know.' She went on to tell Grace about the little scene she'd had with her husband's girl-friend. 'She was furious about our marriage,' Liz added un-necessarily.

'I'll bet she was. Lord, what a hilarious situation! It doesn't sound real.'

'It was real enough,' returned Liz grimly. 'She said she and Nigel were practically engaged before he came to England.'

Grace filed one long nail thoughtfully.

'You believe that?'

Liz shook her head.

'Nigel had told me he never wanted to marry.' A moment's silence and then, slowly, 'Nigel didn't marry me for the money, Grace. He had known all along that the wills were invalid. He came to England for the sole purpose of consulting me – or one of my family – with a view to contesting them.' Grace was looking puzzled, naturally, and Liz went on to explain the whole.

'Then why did he marry you?' Grace looked keenly at her, the nail file idle in her hand.

'That's what I've been trying to figure out ever since Spiros told me—' Liz stopped suddenly as, intruding into her mind, came Nigel's implication that his cousin did not know what he was talking about. At the time she had passed it off, but now she frowned in concentration, wondering why her husband's words should return at this particular time. She sighed audibly. 'Have you any ideas?' she inquired in tones of exasperated confusion.

Grace remained reflectively silent and Liz looked up. The nail file came into use again, but Grace remained deep in thought.

'I have,' she murmured at length, avoiding Liz's gaze, 'but I doubt if it's the correct one.'

Liz glanced up.

'Well, spill it. Any idea's better than none.'

'That day ... you never mentioned much about it. I heard from someone else that Nigel insisted on kissing you in private.'

'Well, what of it?' Liz flushed at the memory and a shaft of anger swept through her.

'What happened?' queried Grace, watching her keenly.

A small hesitant shrug and then,

'He took his pennyworth,' Liz almost snapped.

'You didn't enjoy the experience, apparently.'

'I didn't enjoy any of the kisses!'

'But Nigel's — was it — different from the others?' Grace's expression was a mingling of interest and amusement.

Different? No question about that!

'The man was insufferable!' The retort came swift and sharp and Grace's eyes took on an even more observant expression. 'What is this all about, anyway?' added Liz testily. 'I thought you had an idea as to the reason for Nigel's marrying me?'

A silence fell on the room for one contemplative moment before Grace said quietly,

'You don't suppose he – he fell in love with you that day—?'

'In love?' Liz stared wordlessly at her for several astounded seconds. 'You must be crazy! What sort of an idea's that to put forward? I thought you had something feasible in mind.'

Grace laughed, automatically glancing at the clock. Only ten minutes to dinner time.

'The idea might not be what suits you, Liz, but it is feasible. Nigel wouldn't be the first man to fall in love with you on sight, would he now?' The way Grace cocked an eyebrow was so reminiscent of a similar mannerism of Nigel's that a swift frown darkened Liz's brow.

'Don't be silly!'

'Naturally you're modest,' returned Grace mildly. 'But what I've just said is true, nevertheless, and you know it.'

'Well, Nigel didn't fall in love with me on sight,' rejoined Liz firmly. 'He detests me as much as I detest him!'

Grace swivelled round again and took a lipstick from the glass shelf of her dressing-table.

'You haven't told me what he's like to live with.' Not much expression in Grace's voice; she watched her friend through the mirror as she applied the lipstick.

'We fight all the time.'

'Fight?' repeated Grace after dwelling on this for a

second or two. 'Who wins?' she added curiously and, in Liz's opinion, irrelevantly.

'Who would you expect to win?' she countered.

Grace laughed.

'Now you've set me a poser. In the ordinary way – you. But Nigel ...' Ruefully she shook her head. 'I wouldn't back you against a man like that even though I've seen so little of him.'

A compression of her friend's lips brought another laugh from Grace.

'He receives as good as he gives,' flashed Liz, rising from the bed and taking a powder compact from her handbag. 'And he always will.' Brave words, born of her innate strength of character. But although she hoped to deceive Grace Liz could not deceive herself. She had had proof enough of her husband's superiority even before his final act of mastery.

'Do you enjoy fighting with him?' Grace stood up and moved away so that Liz could use the mirror.

'It relieves the monotony.'

'You know,' said Grace meditatively, 'I ought to be feeling sorry for you – but I'm not.'

'Pity's the last thing I want from anyone.' Liz applied a powder puff to her cheek.

'Frankly, I believe it's the last thing you need.' Grace slipped out of the dress she wore and put another over her head.

Liz said at length, with difficulty,

'I believe you're half expecting us to – to make a go of the marriage?'

'I'm still wondering why Nigel married you.' Grace stretched over her shoulder and completed the fastening of her zip. 'Were I in your place I'd be doing a little experimenting in order to find out.'

'Experimenting?'

Grace looked squarely at her.

'Could you love him? – if he happened to love you?'

Liz glanced away, wondering why she could not voice a swift and emphatic 'no!' to her friend's forthright question. At length she spoke, taking cover once again in evasion.

'Your question's superfluous, because Nigel does not happen to love me.'

'Liz,' said Grace with released asperity, 'Nigel married you for some reason, and that reason could very well be love. Why should he have chosen this way instead of the obvious one of contesting the wills? He must have wanted you, otherwise he'd have gone ahead with his original intention and discussed the contesting of those stupid wills.' Liz had gone a little pale, but she could not speak and Grace continued, 'Experiment, as I've advised. In other words, let him know that you're very different from what you appear to be—'

'Different?'

'You are, Liz. The front you insist on showing to the world is not your real self. You deliberately hide the qualities which you know will appeal to a man – that's because you've never been interested in marrrying, of course, and so you haven't wished to reveal any appealing characteristics. But you're interested in Nigel ... and no matter how much you deny that I wouldn't believe you.'

Strangely Liz made no protest to this outspoken pronouncement – because, at last, she was admitting it was true; she was accepting the pointers instead of obstinately denying them – instead of refusing to own to the real significance of those stirrings of emotion which had first become manifest on the day Nigel had taken her to the Sanctuary. Yes, she *was* interested in Nigel. But not for anything would she admit this to Grace and, with her inherent understanding and tact, Grace pursued the matter no further but instead made the prosaic remark that they ought to be going down to dinner, and opened the bedroom door, inviting Liz to precede her.

'You know Daniel, don't you?' Mrs. Lunn looked from Liz to the smiling young man who had also been invited to dinner. Liz nodded but held out a hand. Daniel had been one of her admirers in the old days but, like the others, he had soon decided that Liz's formidable character was something with which he had no desire to live. Nevertheless, he was perfectly affable to her during dinner, but later when they were sitting a little apart from the others he asked, not without a hint of amusement,

'How's marriage suiting you? I never ever expected you to fall in love.'

She smiled to herself.

'Women are unpredictable,' she merely answered, driving away the intrusion of her husband and of the question which naturally attracted in its wake Grace's assertion, and her own secret admission that she was interested in Nigel. 'Men are too,' she found herself murmuring, rather to her surprise.

'Your husband must be a brave man,' laughed Daniel bluntly, and Liz responded to his laughter.

'Braver than you, Daniel.'

'Braver than a dozen I could mention.' A small pause and then, 'He's a Greek, I believe, and Greeks are notorious for keeping their women under, yet I can't for the life of me see you being kept under.'

'Nor I,' she promptly retorted, sparkling.

'Well,' sighed Daniel, 'it's obviously working, so one of you must be climbing down.'

A wry smile rose involuntarily to Liz's mouth, but she merely said,

'If you're fishing for information, Daniel, then you're wasting your time. I don't discuss my marriage with other men.'

He shrugged.

'Fair enough. Just thought it would be entertaining to hear about it. There has been much talk, as you can very well imagine.'

'Am I so notorious, then?' she asked carelessly.

'Your formidableness is well-known; you're fully aware of that.'

Liz glanced over to where Grace was sitting on the couch with Ray. They were two of a kind, she thought, neither would try to domineer over the other. So they would get along fine, the relationship being satisfactory to them both. Two of a kind. She and Nigel were two of a kind, but even if they fell in love with one another Liz could not see their marriage working. Both were too headstrong and as neither would climb down, as Daniel had termed it, there would not be even the remotest possibility of success.

'When are you going back?' Daniel interrupted her thoughts and she brought her eyes from the contemplation of her friend and looked at her companion. He was smoking a cigarette, and as she watched he drew on it and inhaled deeply.

'A week on Friday; I came for a fortnight.' She would stay as long as she liked, she had asserted, but five minutes before the taxi came to take her to the airport Nigel had said,

'Don't forget, a fortnight and no longer.'

His arrogant command naturally brought a fiery flush to her cheeks and she had said, even though she did wonder if she meant it,

'I'll stay away a month if it suits me!'

'I don't think so. If you're not back here in a fortnight I'll come and fetch you – and,' he added, a glint of warning in his eyes, 'if you put me to that trouble you'll regret it for a devil of a long while!'

'You couldn't drag me back,' she flung at him even as the taxi-driver stood with the door in his hand, having already put her luggage into the cab.

'No,' admitted Nigel, amused now and faintly mocking. 'That's true, but somehow, Liz, I feel sure you'd come quite meekly.' And then, laughing at her explosive expression, he said placatingly and, she thought, rather gently, 'Enjoy yourself, my dear, and remember me to the deaf and dumb school.' And he actually blew her a kiss as the taxi rounded the bend in the drive before disappearing from his vision.

He knew she would come back in the time he had stipulated, and Liz had known. If only she could be a little more pliable, she thought, she and Nigel might after all, get along. But pliability meant weakness, and where men were concerned any form of weakness on a wife's part led automatically to subjection. No, that sort of existence was not for her. No man, not even one with the strength of character of Nigel, was going to subject her to his mastery.

'I expect you find this country dull after the glamour of Greece?' Daniel was saying, and Liz nodded absently.

'I miss the sun, and the scenery. Delphi's a marvellous place.' Her dilatory tone livened to enthusiasm as she spoke and Daniel smiled.

'I ought to come for a holiday,' he said tentatively, and added, 'Would you put me up?'

She looked at him, thinking of Nigel, and his attitude

towards Spiros, right from the first. She could not see him agreeing to put Daniel up at his house. And yet why shouldn't she have a friend over from England if she wished? With a swift return of her sense of superiority and independence she said yes, she would willingly put Daniel up if he decided to come over on a visit.

'When would you be coming?' she wanted to know, and he laughed then, and asked why she was so eager.

That somehow brought a glint to her eye and she found she no longer cared for the idea of his coming over to stay with her and Nigel in Delphi. But he was fired with the idea, it seemed, because he went on to say,

'I have my holidays next month – at the end. I'd love to come; you and your husband could show me around. It would be far preferable to going on my own. One misses all the local colour on a package tour.'

He continued to talk about the holiday and although Liz was still far from being enamoured with the idea she did not now see how she could retract. However, she concluded in the end that he would forget all about it once she had left the country again and so she allowed him to enthuse until he himself became tired of the subject.

She leant back on the couch. Mr. and Mrs. Lunn were chatting together, and so were Grace and Ray. Liz gave a deep sigh. She was so bored and yet she did not know why. Daniel was quite good company; the wine was good and from a record player over in one corner drifted the soft and soothing strains of the *Waltz of the Flowers* from Tchaikovsky's *Nutcracker Suite*. The whole atmosphere and the company were conducive to a pleasant evening of contentment, so why should she be bored? The question was superfluous. Liz knew that it was Nigel's company she wanted, so why pretend? Strangely the admission brought a softness to her features, a sort of tenderness never seen on her face before.

What of Nigel, though? He could have married her for love, Grace had hinted. Then several incidents came flooding back to Liz's mind – Nigel's saying Spiros did not know what he was talking about, then those touches of advice when Nigel had told Liz to think, and she might guess at the truth . . . This in reply to her question, why had he married her? If he did love her, could they make a go of the marriage? Theirs was no longer an unnatural relationship, for Liz felt convinced that that one night was only the beginning, not the end.

'Can I take you home?' Daniel asked later when Liz and he and Ray were preparing to go.

'My car should be here at eleven o'clock,' she smiled. 'Thank you all the same, Daniel.'

'Then let me have your address and I'll write and let you know when I'm coming.' He brought out a small diary and, turning to a page at the back, he waited, pen in hand. She had no alternative than to give her address to him, but she silently prayed he would change his mind. 'Thanks. I'll look forward to seeing you.' His manner and his smile troubled her as she drove home through the storm that had broken as they all left Liz's house. She should not have been so impulsive as to invite him, she concluded, for she had a strong suspicion that he would not change his mind about the suggested visit. However, the damage was done now, so there was nothing to be gained by teasing herself with it.

CHAPTER EIGHT

To Liz's astonishment Nigel was at the airport to meet her when her plane landed. She had told him the time of her arrival, but had fully expected to have to take a taxi home.

The little thrill of pleasure his appearance afforded her was of course hidden, but the blush that rose to her cheeks as the result of recollection was there for him to see, and his eyes twinkled in amusement. She bristled. If only he would not be so infuriatingly superior, she thought, for it was patently clear that he guessed the reason for her swift rise of colour.

'How is everyone at home?' he inquired affably as he drove her from the airport. 'Still in the pink of condition, I hope?'

'Gran isn't,' answered Liz rather sadly. 'But then it's only to be expected. She had a fall and I had to call in the doctor.'

'What did he say?'

'It's her heart – and she has rheumatism, of course. I'm afraid she's going to be helpless quite soon.' Again sadness entered her voice and Nigel turned swiftly.

'You think a lot about her, don't you?'

She nodded.

'Old people worry me – and especially Great-Gran. We've always got on so well together.'

A small pause and then,

'Well, Liz, you've done your duty by them all. They'd have been in a home but for you.' She said nothing and after passing a slow vehicle he spoke again. 'Do you still consider it a sacrifice?' His lazy drawl was edged with amusement and although she tried to remain amicable and calm she found herself wanting to return him some scathing report. Why couldn't he be a little more flexible and — humble, even? That thought led to a smile. The man would not understand the meaning of the word!

'You yourself don't appear to be perturbed by my sacrifice, as you call it.'

'Why should I be? You made the decision, knowing what it entailed.'

'Knowing what it entailed?' she gasped, then wished she had held a rein on her tongue because of his sudden gust of laughter and the slanting glance of mockery he cast at her.

'No, of course you didn't, did you? All was to be nice and platonic – and would have been, Liz, had you not goaded me so often.'

'Do you mind changing the subject?' she snapped, adding, 'I'm already beginning to wish I'd stayed at home a little longer!'

'I wonder ...' He changed gear and stayed behind a lorry. 'Tell me about your visit. What did you do with your time?' Nigel smiled at her as he asked the question.

'I went out on several occasions, to friends. But for the most part I stayed in. I had a feeling I might never see Gran again.'

'Did you miss me?' he asked after a moment's silence.

The pomposity of the man! How could she ever have contemplated being more friendly? She had even gone as far as to contemplate the possibility of trying to make a success of the marriage. She must have been out of her mind.

'I did not! It was wonderful to get away from you for a while.'

'Thanks,' laconically. 'I wish I hadn't bothered to come and pick you up.'

'If my company annoys you there's a remedy. You can drop me just whenever you like. There are plenty of taxis available.'

He drew an exasperated breath.

'Be careful, Liz, for I might do just that.' He cut out to pass the lorry and then increased his speed.

'Do you derive pleasure from these arguments?' she inquired coldly, her patience stretched to the limit.

'A certain amount,' he owned with humour. 'You see, I've never met a girl like you before. You're quite unique. Of course,' he added thoughtfully, 'had you not been, you'd have been married long before I met you.'

'What exactly do you mean by that remark?'

'Obviously you were too formidable for the local lads – a challenge none was willing to accept.'

'You were, though.' Curiosity took the place of the tang in her voice.

'I felt myself capable of taming you.' With a deft touch of the wheel he swerved to avoid a cyclist who was barely visible among the load he carried on his back and on the carrier and handlebars of the bicycle.

'I wonder if you know just how pompous you are. It's not difficult to see why *you* were not married before you met me!'

He laughed.

'I could have been,' he commented mildly. 'Although you'll never believe that.'

'Yes, I will – in fact, I take it back. Greta would have been misguided enough to have you. I often wonder why you didn't marry her.'

'She was not unique, Liz, that's why I didn't marry her.'

'Is that the only reason?' Liz turned her head and sent him a glance from under her lashes.

'What other reason could there be?' he countered.

'It's said that a Greek never marries his pillow friend.'

He considered that.

'Had you been my pillow friend I most certainly would have married you,' he replied with some amusement.

Her eyes narrowed. So his reason for marrying her *was* desire – or so it would seem. With an ironical twist of her lips she recalled what Grace had said about the probability of his marrying her for love.

'Am I supposed to regard that as flattery?' she inquired with sarcasm.

'It was flattery, my girl, and you know it.'

She flushed, but said,

'So I do appeal to you in – in some ways?'

He waited a moment, then said, with taunting amusement,

'You were going to say "in one way", weren't you?'

'All right,' she retorted. 'As long as we're being so outspoken – I appeal to your baser instincts, is that right?'

He frowned in pain and said with a sort of mild irritability,

'How indelicate you are – and what a term! I have never considered the natural instincts as base.' She turned sharply away and fell into a contemplation of the view. Across a limpid crystalline sea the rocky heights of the islands of Salamis and Aegina cut irregularly into the vivid sapphire of a Grecian sky, naked in contrast to the verdure of the lower slopes of Aegina, clothed with olives and figs and vines. Nigel merely laughed at her withdrawal and presently continued, an edge of mockery to his words, 'I wonder what you'd say were I to deny that you appeal to me – in one way?'

She caught her breath in fury.

'Once again, can we change the subject?'

'You brought it up,' he reminded her blandly.

She sighed.

'Perhaps I had better take a taxi. Stop the car here and I'll get out.'

For an answer he increased his speed and they drove for miles and miles without speaking a word. But as they neared the *khani* where Nigel had stopped on the occasion of his first bringing her up here he slowed down and asked Liz if she wanted a drink.

This time she was a little wiser than before.

'Yes, please.'

One or two men sprawled at another table, but the *cafeneion* was very peaceful and quiet and Liz and Nigel sat under a spreading tree and drank coffee and iced water.

'I'm sorry, Liz,' he said suddenly and unexpectedly. 'I suppose I just can't resist teasing you—'

'Teasing?' She raised her brows, but she smiled too, and her husband responded.

'What name do you have for it, then?' he inquired with affable interest.

'Taunting – goading – provoking.'

He laughed.

'We'll call a truce, just for today?' He cocked her a glance. 'I've missed you, Liz, and I'm willing to admit it. Life before I knew you must have been devilishly dull.'

Her eyes widened with surprise.

He had never before lowered his pride this way and Liz

felt she should make some small concession herself, but she had much more difficulty than he, and into her silence he spoke, a trifle impatiently.

'Drop the cloak for once, Liz. Let me see what you're really like.'

'I don't know what you mean?'

'Be honest. Certainly you know what I mean. There's another side to you altogether. Why you persist in hiding it I don't know.'

Recollection brought back a similar assertion which Grace had made and Liz reddened.

'I'm no feminine softie, if that's what you're hoping.'

'Indeed, no. A feminine softie would bore me to distraction! What fun is there in life if one can subdue without a fight?' he added in some amusement. 'A man worth his salt welcomes resistance.'

She had to laugh.

'If I'm unique, then you are too.' She leant forward to take up her coffee from the table.

'Two of a kind, Liz,' he murmured, watching her over the rim of his cup. And he added, 'Must we fight to the end – or are you going to show me the other side?'

'So the other side, as you call it, is a weak side?' she challenged, a sparkle in her eyes.

'Not at all. You're saying that womanliness and weakness are synonymous, which is ridiculous, simply because womanliness is natural and weakness is not. A woman can be natural without being weak.' He cocked an eyebrow. 'Logical, you'll agree?'

Again she had to laugh.

'Are you trying to tie me up in knots, Nigel?' Her eyes were on his face, and something caught at a thread within her, jerking it so that she seemed to be left in a state of unbalance. Undeniably he was handsome! And it was difficult to remain immune to his profound attractiveness as a man, especially with her newly-found emotions clamouring for freedom to grow and expand.

Nigel gave her a faintly admonishing look.

'You'll not give an inch, will you?'

Why couldn't she respond to this attractive mood of his? – and drop all antagonism? That she wanted to could not be denied and a rueful smile touched her lips.

'Supposing I did give an inch,' she queried warily. 'What sort of situation would I find myself in?'

'A most happy one,' he responded without the slightest hesitation, and Liz gave a visible start. Gentle colour flecked each lovely cheek, and her lips, parted slightly, quivered on the invitation of a kiss.

'What are you saying to me, Nigel?'

He opened his mouth, then closed it again, and she realized with a little sinking feeling that she would never know what he had been going to say before, with a swift glance at her, he changed his mind.

'Perhaps I'm saying that we might get along in a more comfortable way?' His dark unsmiling face was firm and hard. She wondered at his change of mood, and tried to find the reason for it. Had he been about to declare his love – but then drawn back, just as an enemy would draw back, deceiving his adversary into an advance that would bring him closer, and make him more vulnerable? Liz studied her husband, her every nerve alert and on the defensive. That she cared she would not now deny, but if caring meant subjugation then it must be cautiously hidden.

Nigel met her gaze and a half smile touched the firm outline of his mouth. Did he guess her thoughts? she wondered, lowering her lashes as the idea formed. She would never tell him now how she felt – not unless he himself displayed some weakness, or revealed in some way his intention of regarding her always as an equal.

Someone put on a record and a man at the next table, having been sprawled in an attitude of sleepy indolence, sprang up from his chair and began to dance. This was a regular occurrence, even if there were no tourists about. Greek men danced for the sheer joy of living, and their vigour while thus engaged was incredible. They leapt and twisted and sprang, putting every ounce of energy they possessed into whichever dance they were performing, whether it be slow and graceful or wild and orgiastic.

But to Liz these dancing men were still much of a novelty and while she was engrossed in the incredible movements going on before her Nigel's eyes were idly taking in every change in her expression, and he gave a little sigh, which brought her head round. His eyes took on a mocking light then, and he said, his deep voice brisk and faintly commanding,

'Are you ready? It's time we were on our way.'

That evening, after dinner when they were out on the verandah, a quietness enveloped them both; they were deep in their own thoughts. It was a clear still night, unlit by the moon, but the purple vault above was bright with stars which rolled through the slow-moving cumulus cloud that had gathered since dusk over the stark massif of Parnassus.

Scents hung on the still air and as the silent moments passed a sense of peace came over Liz which she had seldom before experienced. Yet, paradoxically, the very serenity disturbed her, because she was so conscious of Nigel's presence and the sheer masculine strength of him. In addition there seemed to be some subtle interchange of mind, some sweet and intimate communion between them. It could not be ignored any more than her own senses could be ignored – senses vibrant and alive to the power her husband was beginning to gain over her.

He seemed to sense her feelings and looked at her, his features softened by the opaline shadows in which he sat.

'Tell me your thoughts, Liz?' Softly persuasive the tones – and yet imperious.

It was not possible to answer and she shook her head. She smiled, though, and he responded. Liz asked,

'Do you feel like a stroll?'

His smile deepened.

'Safer to walk, you think?' he quizzed.

'Such a thought never entered my mind.'

'In that case, my dear, you are blissfully unaware of the danger.'

'Danger?' She cast him a frowning glance.

'I could, my dear, make love to you right here,' he told her with some amusement. 'That one taste whetted my appetite, and you've been gone from me for a fortnight.'

Her frown darkened. The thought of approaching night had naturally been with her for some time and she had almost reached the stage when she could have gone to her husband willingly, but now he had spoiled everything and resentment flared – resentment and anger and the determination to resist him.

'If you've managed without me for a fortnight then you can continue to do so,' she snapped, aware of disappointment at this turn which he had deliberately brought about. Why was he so infuriatingly awkward?

He stood up, and snapped on a light; it fell full on her lovely face and Nigel stared down at her, his eyes dark and filmed with inflexibility and desire.

'How little you understand me, Liz. You should know you can't go on forever resisting me. No, don't interrupt.

I'm not a fool; I know full well I awakened a desire in you ... I know, Liz, that although you will instantly deny it, you did in fact enjoy my lovemaking.'

Her eyes blazed. Why couldn't he be more subtle? — more diplomatic? He enjoyed riling her, that was it, and she was fool enough to allow herself to be riled. If only she could assume an icy indifference, as she had several times promised herself she would, then perhaps she could wear him down and he would desist from this attitude of taunting mockery.

'What an opinion you have of yourself!' she cried. 'And why did you say we'd call a truce when all the time you harbour this urge to provoke me?' She did not want her disappointment to quiver on the edge of her voice, but it did — and her husband noticed and his face softened as with a gentle persuasive gesture he reached for her hand.

'Am I a fool, I wonder?' he murmured almost to himself. 'Is it that I have broken through your reserve and don't know it?' She glinted at him, but he ignored it as he added in a quiet voice, 'Take my hand, Liz.'

The moment was profound, fraught with suspense ... because Liz knew she wanted nothing more than to capitulate, and yet she said, ignoring his hand,

'I'm too honest to affect submission, Nigel. I am what I am — a woman who has no intention of accepting any man's authority over her.'

With a little smothered oath he grasped at her hand, and then she was in his arms, her lips possessed, her resisting body strained to his, and kept there.

'We'll not walk, after all,' he said a moment later. 'It's too late.'

Her teeth came together.

'I'm walking, no matter what you say!'

141

'Alone?' Nigel took a step away from her.

'I'm not afraid of the dark,' she returned with strong derision, and a laugh escaped him.

'Not afraid of anything, are you?' A pause for her to comment, but she turned away from him, furious because her mouth was bruised and her body trembled from his strength and mastery. 'Shall I put fear into you? Will that bring you down? I *can* put fear into you, Liz, so don't adopt that attitude. I've warned you that I'm not a patient man, and my tolerance is nothing to speak of either. I've reached the stage when the primitive instinct predominates. I have a strong urge to break you – no matter how I do it.' His expression had changed; he appeared ruthless, pagan as the god Hades himself. And although her head was tilted and her eyes militant – oh, she did feel a trembling sensation inside her! The acknowledgement of this only served to increase her anger and she made for the steps leading off the verandah. An encircling vice on her wrist arrested her progress and she swung round, her eyes ablaze.

'Let go of me!'

'You vixen, Liz.' His voice was amused, but softly dangerous; his hold remained firm on her wrist. 'You talk about provocation ... My dear Liz, you are the one who provokes. You're a challenge which, on first deciding to marry you, I knew I would enjoy meeting—' His mouth found hers again and she knew the fire of his passion and fought desperately against it. But the next moment he had lifted her off her feet; she felt the rapid beating of his heart against her and his warm breath on her face as, with no more effort than if he carried a doll, Nigel took her into the house ...

A week later, having been away for three days, Nigel informed Liz that they would be attending a party which was being held on Dendras's yacht which was moored in the harbour at Mandraki in Rhodes.

'It will last three or four days,' he told her, 'so you'll require lots of clothes.'

They were in the lounge, having afternoon tea, and Liz glanced away, searching for some answer that would aggravate him. But all she found to say was,

'I've no wish to come with you.'

'I can't go alone, Liz,' he returned quietly.

'Then take Greta—' The words were out before she could stem them and she lowered her lashes to mask her expression. If he should take Greta ... What would she, Liz, feel like? But of course he would not take Greta, not to his friend's yacht.

Nigel's eyes had darkened at her unthinking rejoinder and his mouth went tight.

'You are coming with me,' he said in dangerously quiet tones. 'So let's have no more childish refusals or pettish threats. You should know me sufficiently well by now to be sure I'll retaliate.'

'You can't drag me to this yacht!'

'You'll fly to the island with me.' The same quiet tones, the same film of danger covering them. He seemed so triumphant, so very sure of himself ... and of her. Yes, when he had so confidently asserted that she had enjoyed his lovemaking he knew what he was talking about. He still held her, and although she fumed inwardly, condemning her inability to resist, she at the same time owned that life without Nigel would not now hold very much at all. Had he won merely by making himself desirable to her? – as she was undoubtedly desirable to him? The idea caused her to wince and squirm and endeavour to thrust it from her. She had never wanted love – much less had she wanted sex. And for her to be forced to own that Nigel as a lover appealed to her so strongly that he actually held her a prisoner was something to which she could become resigned only with the passing of time. For the present, the discovery was so new and, therefore, so distasteful, that she felt that all there was between her husband and herself was lust – an insatiable desire for each other's bodies.

There had been several clashes between them since that night, so short a time ago, when he had literally forced her to his will, for in her fury and refusal to be overcome she had fought him as tigress would fight in defending her young. But to no avail, as she knew it could not be. She was no match for Nigel in any mood, but in the mood of that night she was utterly helpless. For it was not only his desire that urged him to subdue her but also her own refusal to succumb quietly, her struggles having fired off a primeval urge to conquer her completely.

'When is this party?' she asked with sudden abruptness.

'Not for another three weeks. You have plenty of time to prepare for it.'

She was interested, in spite of herself.

'Do your friends often have parties on their yachts?'

His fine lips twitched at that.

'Dendras is the only one who owns a yacht – and he wouldn't own that if it weren't for Nicoleta's money.'

'So the others aren't as wealthy?'

He shook his head, glancing up as a huge flying beetle came through the open window. Liz shuddered, but Nigel only smiled and said,

'It'll go out again in a moment.'

'You—?' She glanced at him. 'Have you never thought of having a yacht?' She was really sounding him to discover just how wealthy he was, and he smiled at her, his brows lifted in an air of faint mockery.

'I can afford one, if that's what you're wanting to know ...' He fell silent as she blushed and then added, softly, 'And I don't require help from my wife.' Her eyes flashed; this led to laughter on his part and a swift, 'No, my dear, I know I wouldn't receive any help from you. Isn't that what you were about to say?'

His quick perception eroded her temper and she flashed,

'How clever you are! Omniscient, in fact!'

Nigel leant back, eyes laughing, his light grey jacket contrasting attractively with the deep red Italian brocatelle with which the chair was covered.

'No, my dear, certainly not omniscient,' he denied with faint satire. 'Had I been that I should have known what I was in for.'

'And you didn't?' she asked, diverted and surprised.

He shook his head, and the laughter lines at the sides of his eyes deepened until they were etchings of attractiveness which brought unwanted flutterings to her breast.

'I didn't,' was Nigel's mock grim rejoinder.

'And if you had,' she challenged, 'would you have acted differently?' Having anticipated the question Nigel was shaking his head long before she had finished speaking.

'You know very well I wouldn't, Liz,' he chided gently. 'You are the one for me and I knew it the moment I set eyes on you ... Two of a kind, remember what I said?' He was laughing at her, as he so often laughed at her.

'What a pity I didn't have the sense to know about those wills, as you did,' she murmured, but only because she was interested in his reaction – certainly not because she regretted the marriage. Nigel was right, they were two of a kind, and although it looked very much as if they were to spend the rest of their lives fighting, they would remain together. Liz had no doubts about that, not now that she had accepted the fact that her own need of Nigel was as great as his need of her.

'What a lot we'd both have missed. No, my dear, don't go wishing that you'd been wiser – not that it would do any good now,' he added with an amused smile.

'You would have continued that peaceful well-organized life you once mentioned,' she returned with the merest hint of mischief.

Nigel frowned in thought.

'Peaceful and well-organized ... Is that how I described it?' he asked her curiously, and she nodded.

'Those were your very words.'

'I did say, more recently, that life must have been dull until you came into it. Odd how we consider ourselves to be content, to possess all that goes to make life comfortable and full – and then suddenly something happens and the astounding truth is flashed at you and you discover that life is merely a dull and aimless round after all.' He was reflecting, musing to himself as if he had forgotten Liz's presence altogether.

'Surely *your* life was no dull and aimless round.' Deliberately she broke in on his reverie and he glanced up. 'You had your money and your friends ... and Greta,' she could not help adding, brought to that particular piece of malice by some irritating, compelling force within her. His gaze became penetrating; his half stifled intake of breath was in itself a tacit reproach even before he admonished,

'You're what other women would call a bitch, Liz. Why don't you make some effort at control?'

She reddened but, strangely, found no withering retort ready to fly to her lips.

'There's no need to become personal, Nigel.' And although she endeavoured to inject some sort of protest into her voice she found to her disgust that, on the contrary, she was subdued and in fact faintly apologetic. What had this man done to her? Was it his aim to break her spirit? The idea should by rights have set her temper alight, but she was beginning to wonder if, at some distant date, Nigel would in fact break her spirit. If he did it would be only because of the way she was now feeling about him, and should this feeling grow and grow how could she continue to combat both her husband's superior strength and his inordinate attraction for her?

'You brought the personal angle into it,' he reminded her, his eyes glinting, hard as obsidian, if not quite as dark. 'Greta is of the past. You and I are concerned only with the present and the future.'

'You're sure she's of the past?' Swift the query and Nigel faintly smiled.

'Jealous, maybe?' he quizzed, and her flush deepened and fluctuated and her beautiful lashes swept down to throw shadows that concealed her expression.

'What an excessive amount of self-conceit you possess! Why should I be jealous of your mistress!'

'My one-time mistress,' he corrected, and she winced at the admission even though she had no illusions about the role Greta had played in her husband's life. And Greta wouldn't have been the only one, Liz surmised, for Nigel was no different from any other man.

Liz looked down at her hands, feeling unhappy and, oddly, quite alone. They had finished their tea and she rose from her chair.

'I'm going to sit outside and read,' she said a trifle huskily. 'It's a shame to be in; I expect the rains will be coming soon.' Her change of the subject at this crucial point spoke for itself and with unexpected perception and gentleness Nigel reached out and took her hand in his.

'Greta is of the past, Liz,' he repeated softly and, rising, tilted her face and placed a gentle kiss upon her lips.

CHAPTER NINE

To Liz's dismay Daniel wrote a week later to say he was coming over for a fortnight.

'I'll be leaving on the fifteenth,' he ended, and told Liz not to bother writing back. He was leaving England in a couple of days as he intended spending a few days in Venice before coming on to them.

Liz was annoyed, but with herself. In a sudden fit of defiance she had said Daniel could come over and stay with her. She had thought at the time that Nigel might not be home anyway, but she now felt convinced that from now on her husband would be away from home only when it was absolutely necessary. Well, he'd have to be told, she supposed, and as there seemed nothing to be gained by a delay she went along to his study door and knocked.

'Come in.' He was absorbed in work, perusing some papers on his desk, a pen in one hand. But he smiled on seeing who had entered and gestured towards a chair. 'What is it, Liz?'

How to begin? Liz cursed herself for her stupid act of defiance.

'When I was at home I invited a friend over to stay,' she began, then stopped on seeing her husband's expression.

'You never mentioned this. When is she coming?'

Liz coughed to clear her throat.

'It's Daniel Westcliffe – an old friend.'

A small silence; Nigel stared darkly at her through half-closed eyes.

'Friend – or flame?' he inquired mildly at last.

A rush of anger sped through her.

'He's my friend! And I've invited him to stay here. I hope you've no objections!'

Another silence followed. Nigel's face became engraved with suppressed anger.

'And if I have?' he queried gently.

'It'll be too bad, because there's no way of putting him off. He's having a stay in Venice before coming on here. I received his letter only a few minutes ago.'

'You would have put him off?' Nigel watched her oddly.

'No,' she returned promptly, and Nigel's eyes darkened. 'I invited him to come – and I'm looking forward to his visit.'

'When is he arriving?'

'On Thursday.'

'How long is he staying?'

'A fortnight—'

'A fortnight? Have you forgotten we're leaving here in a fortnight's time?'

'Daniel will leave the day before we do.'

Nigel looked at her, his eyes like steel, his mouth set in a firm inflexible line which troubled Liz in spite of her determination to make a firm stand.

'Why didn't you mention this – er – friend of yours?' he demanded, dropping the pen on the desk and leaning back in his chair. 'What's the idea of springing it on me at the last moment?'

'I haven't sprung it on you—' She broke off as he raised his eyebrows, but as he made no comment she continued, 'I thought he might not come – people say these things and often don't mean them.'

'But if you invite someone over, and they accept – and

obviously this Daniel did accept – then it's to be expected that he'll come. Are you sure you can't put him off?' Nigel asked with suspicion.

On the point of saying that a letter would not arrive in time Liz stopped herself. Such a statement would be tantamount to admitting that she had regretted her invitation and that she was not now keen on Daniel's coming to stay with them.

'I don't want to put him off. I'm looking forward to having him here.'

A deep sigh escaped Nigel. He said curtly,

'I suppose you have every right to invite your friends – as this is your home,' he remarked, surprising her by his reasonable manner, for she felt certain he was still furious. 'However, he can't stay the full fortnight—'

'I'm not sending him off to an hotel!'

Her husband's eyes glinted.

'He's not staying here until the very moment of our departure. You'll explain, and he'll understand.'

Liz shook her head determinedly.

'He's staying here,' she said obstinately. 'It would be the height of ill manners to ask him, as I have done, and then send him to an hotel.'

'It would be for a couple of days only.' Soft tones but inflexible. Liz drew an angry breath and said,

'There's no necessity for that. I can't see any reason for your attitude.'

'You'll require time to organize yourself. You have shopping to do, the hairdresser to visit—' He shook his head. 'No, Liz, your friend may stay about ten days and that's all.' Nigel came forward in his chair and took up his pen again. 'And now, if you'll leave me, I have work to do.'

His quiet authoritative way, the very act of picking up

the pen ... Liz fumed, but stood up and turned to the door.

'He's staying a fortnight,' she said over her shoulder, and would have left the room before Nigel could retort, but he was on his feet and even as she put out a hand to open the door he had caught it and she was roughly swung around to face him.

'If you're not damned careful,' he almost snarled, 'this Daniel will get no further than the doorstep! Think yourself lucky I'm agreeable to his coming at all ... and leave it at that.' His face drew close, dark and menacing and etched in granite. 'My patience, Liz,' he murmured, scarcely above a whisper. 'For your own sake don't try it too far.'

'If you're threatening me with violence—' she began, but a little shake cut her short.

'There's no "if" about it. I once promised you a bruise or two and by God you'll be lucky if you manage to escape them! Heed my warnings, Liz, or you'll feel my strength in a very different way from what you've ever felt it before.' He released her, noting her white face and the convulsive movement of her lips. 'Anger or fear?' he asked, amused now and faintly mocking. 'You probably don't know it, but you're as white as a sheet.'

In addition she was inwardly trembling, but naturally Liz kept this to herself. With a final act of defiance she tilted her chin and flashed,

'Lay a finger on me and I'll seek protection!'

To her surprise he laughed and said,

'From whom, might I ask?'

'The police.'

Another laugh.

'So confident! My dear, you're in Greece now. The police don't trouble themselves with domestic affairs. If a man wants to beat his wife he gets on with it, and no one interferes. So be advised by me and watch your step.' And with a little shove he had sent her through the door. It closed and she stood glaring at it, her fury a burning vapour suffusing her entire body. If only she could retaliate – and to some effect. For what retaliation she had hitherto put up had proved entirely ineffective. Daniel ... She could humiliate Nigel by flirting with her visitor ... That should bring her imperious, self-opinionated husband down a peg – a few pegs, in fact!

Daniel duly arrived two days later and was introduced to Nigel, who spoke to him with the sort of polite courtesy Liz had expected of him. No warmth, no smile, but that did not surprise Liz. However, these things registered with Daniel and later, on finding herself alone with Liz, he remarked on her husband's lack of enthusiasm, adding,

'He didn't mind my coming? I mean, he isn't the jealous sort, is he?'

She shook her head, but felt it would be most interesting to see how Nigel reacted to her flirting with Daniel.

'No, he isn't jealous. And as for his manner – Nigel isn't the demonstrative sort, Daniel, so you'll have to take him as you find him. He's quite sociable, but that aloofness is there – practically all the time. It's part of his character.'

Daniel shrugged. He and Liz were in the garden, sitting on deck chairs, while Nigel was in his study, having gone there within a few moments of Daniel's arrival.

'This sort of life's a complete change for you.' Daniel looked curiously at Liz. 'Don't you find it quiet?'

She glanced up, and across the garden – which was in itself a paradise of tropical trees and shrubs – to the scene beyond – the gorge and sheer walls of the mountain, the naked peaks where eagles soared and nested, the Sanctuary of Apollo down there below, drowsy in the sunshine. Olive trees, their silver grey leaves fluttering in the breeze, stretched away across the great Plain of Amphissa towards the Gulf of Corinth, its shimmering waters blue and lazy under a sapphire Grecian sky. Liz shook her head. Peace reigned in these mountains, and silence deep and profound. Where, these days, could one find such seclusion? No crowds now because the season was ending, and during the winter months there would scarcely be a soul on the site.

'I do find it quiet,' Liz replied at length, but added, 'I like it, though. One can have too much of the other kind of pleasure – the round of parties and visits.'

'If I remember you never cared for those very much,' Daniel said reflectively. 'But on the other hand you didn't bury yourself as you appear to be doing here.'

She lay back and put her hands behind her, supporting her head.

'I'm not buried, exactly, Daniel. For example, in a couple of weeks' time Nigel and I are going off to Rhodes to stay on a yacht. It belongs to a friend of Nigel's.'

'In a fortnight?' Daniel looked swiftly at her.

'We go the day after you leave, so it's all right,' she assured him. Nigel had asked for it and now he would get it. Had he adopted a more tolerant attitude she would perhaps have explained the position to Daniel, but she now had no intention of doing so, although she did wonder how she would make all her preparations while they had a guest in the house. She could hardly leave him alone, and Nigel would certainly not entertain him.

'Are you sure, Liz?' Daniel seemed a trifle anxious. 'I could leave a couple of days earlier. I wouldn't mind in the least; it would give me a chance to see Athens.'

She hesitated. The problem could be solved – and yet should she accept this offer of Daniel's then Nigel would be sure to conclude that she had bowed meekly to his will. And that Liz could not bear.

'You must stay the full fortnight,' she smiled. 'I shan't be inconvenienced in any way.'

During dinner Nigel exhibited the courtesy which good manners demanded, but later, when he came to Liz's room, he broached the subject of Daniel's departure.

'Did you tell him it wasn't convenient for him to stay the full fortnight?'

Nigel was in his dressing-gown, Liz in her nightdress. She sat at the dressing-table, brushing her hair while Nigel sat on the chair by the window watching her.

'I did not.' She turned as she spoke, interested in his reaction. The brevity of her reply and its swift delivery brought a glint to his eyes, as she fully expected it would.

'We'll see about that, Liz,' was the quiet reply. 'You're just being deliberately awkward,' he added in the same soft inflexible tones. 'You know as well as I that you need some time – a couple of days at least – to prepare for the party.'

'I'll do it while Daniel's here. He won't mind if I leave him to his own devices for a day.'

Nigel stood up, and came towards her. He seemed icily cold and Liz felt a thread of uneasiness run through her body.

'You leave me no alternative than to tell him, straight out, that it's not convenient for him to stay I expect he'll understand, when I've explained the position.'

Her face flushed with anger.

'He's my guest, so you can keep out of it. It would be downright rude to tell him to go.'

Nigel's brow darkened ominously. He was very close and Liz felt her nerves tingle. In another moment, she thought, he would jerk her to her feet and shake her, or bruise her mouth, or give her some other display of his mastery. What a life! And yet ... Liz knew she would not change it even if she could. Something held her to Nigel, something strong and durable, and, strangely, there was an aura of romance about their relationship in spite of all their arguments. For Nigel remained the perfect lover, tender and gentle ... and confidently persuasive. With a deep expressive gaze she watched him through the mirror, breathless and expectant because for some quite unbelievable reason she felt pliable and receptive ... and very feminine. She looked it too, sitting there in an enchanting film of white transparent nylon, her lovely hair in a shining cascade of gold falling on to her golden, naked shoulders. Daniel and any arguments pertaining to him were forgotten; only she and Nigel existed. Through the window night sounds drifted – goat bells and donkeys in the far distance and the droning of nocturnal insects closer to. The floating air transported exotic perfumes into the room, and the subtle illumination from a single rose-shaded lamp lent its contribution to the spell of romance. Liz's eyes shone, and smiled at her husband; her lips quivered and parted, her hands trembled a little and she placed the hairbrush aside, surrender hovering on the edge of her mind ...

She heard Nigel's quick indrawn breath; her excitement grew and she swivelled round and looked up at him. His eyes held hers before roving over her, from her head to her neck and beyond. And then, puzzled, she saw his eyes kindle strangely as if at some secret idea, and the glimmer of a smile suddenly played around his mouth.

'We'll talk about it in the morning.' His face had become a mask of lazy boredom, but although Liz felt a strange prickling of her senses she was totally unprepared for what was to follow. 'I'm tired and I'm sure you are too, so I'll say good night. Sleep well.'

Liz started. Had he uttered words such as those? Could he really leave her? The revelation came as a shock.

'Good night.' She swallowed something hard and bitter in her throat. Never had disappointment swept over her in a deluge such as this. She picked up the brush, but it remained idle in her hand; her lip was caught between her teeth. She released it as she said, 'You're r-right. I am tired.'

Her voice was quivering and frayed; Nigel stepped back abruptly, as if he were pressed by the need for movement.

Stooping, he touched her forehead with his lips. Her eyes met his, but he straightened up and moved away. She had the conviction that not for anything in the world would he allow her to see his expression. A moment later Liz was staring at the closed door, amazed to discover that her eyes were filmed with moisture.

True to his threat Nigel had a word with their guest about the length of his stay. Liz was absent, being upstairs in her room, but when she came down the two men were sitting on the patio and it was clear from the snatch of conversation she heard as she approached them that Daniel had agreed to leave two days before the agreed date of his departure. Liz sent her husband a glinting look, but he merely flicked her an indifferent glance and went on talking to Daniel. Liz sat down, crossing one lovely slender leg over the other. Nigel's attention strayed from Daniel for a space as his eyes roved. Liz flushed, wondering at the sanguine air about him; he seemed like a man who had been experimenting and was waiting to see if his experiment had proved successful. How unfathomable he was! Liz did wish she could probe that mind of his. The infuriating, provoking creature! She hated that smile which seemed to be more mocking than ever this morning, and his eyes laughed at her in a way that challenged even while they gleamed with a sort of gloating satisfaction.

'Nigel's been saying it's not really convenient for me to stay for the full fortnight.' Daniel spoke affably enough and Liz realized he was really rather glad, for this gave him the opportunity of having a couple of days in the capital. His next words confirmed this. 'It would be a waste to come all this way and go back without visiting Athens. So I'll leave here on Tuesday instead of Thursday.'

Meeting Nigel's eyes, Liz saw again the hint of mocking triumph in his expression and her mouth went tight. But of course there could be no brick-slinging before Daniel, but Liz was more determined than ever to humiliate Nigel by flirting with their guest.

For several days Nigel did not seem to notice, and Liz wondered if his indifference was assumed. It was always impossible to read what went on inside that head of his, for he had the easy ability of drawing an impassive mask over his countenance.

During this time he kept to his own room, and this both angered Liz and hurt her. Perhaps he no longer wanted her, she thought, continuing to flirt with Daniel, hoping for some variation in Nigel's reaction. But he remained indifferent, bored, even — certainly not in the least jealous. And then, when Daniel had been with them for just over a week, Nigel announced his intention of going to Athens for a couple of days.

'Is Greta there?' she asked, piqued both by Nigel's keeping to his own room and by his indifference to her flirtations with Daniel.

'As a matter of fact she is,' Nigel replied, yawning. They were on the terrace, Daniel having gone off alone to the Sanctuary.

'You're meeting her?' The question escaped. Liz hadn't really wanted to ask it.

'Undoubtedly we shall meet.' He cocked her a glance of amusement not unmingled with mockery. Her eyes flamed with swiftly-ignited fury. Yet she was close to tears, even though scarcely aware of it herself. Nigel could not possibly know and yet his gaze was extremely odd as he waited for her to speak.

'I hope you enjoy yourselves . . .' And she allowed her voice to fade somewhat before adding, with slow significance, 'As I shall be enjoying myself with Daniel.'

Flint and fire looked out of those grey-green eyes and in spite of her bravado Liz felt her pulse jerk with apprehension. One of these days she would go just that one little step too far, she felt sure. But Nigel did goad her so! His heavy lids drooped as she watched him, and presently he drawled, his change of manner startling her,

'It's fashionable these days for married couples to enjoy themselves with other partners. And so sensible, don't you agree? It obviates the possibility of boredom. One returns to one's spouse refreshed by the change—' He broke off, laughing at her explosive expression, his eyes on her clenched fists. 'What's wrong?' he asked, still amused. 'The practice is agreeable to you . . . judging by what you've just said.' The low-toned inference was sufficiently plain for Liz to guess at once that Nigel trusted her implicitly. He was just playing with her, knowing full well that she had no intention of indulging in a sordid affair with Daniel. Hadn't she once declared she would never be any man's mistress? And hadn't Nigel also stated emphatically that he trusted her? So her veiled threat about having an affair with Daniel had inevitably misfired, Nigel being totally untouched by it – after that first fiery moment, of course. It was she herself who was affected, Nigel having turned the tables on her – although she had paved the way by introducing the subject of Greta. Liz looked squarely at her husband, sitting back in his chair, one hand on the cane arm, the other stroking his chin thoughtfully. Behind him a bougainvillea smouldered against its pillared support, stirring in the breeze so that strange shadows were cast and Nigel's face became obscured. But as the shadows swung with the caprices in the wind his features would again be revealed in all their pagan aspects – the lined and lowering brow, the high cheekbones and thrusting jaw. The crystalline hardness of his eyes was tempered now by a glimmer of boredom, the obdurate set of his lips faintly softened as, moving his hand from his cheek to his mouth, Nigel stifled a yawn. This action inflamed her.

'If you're so bored,' she quivered, 'then why do you trouble to sit here with me?'

A brittle pause before he said, with sudden icy precision,

'You might belong to the British aristocracy, Liz, but your manners leave a great deal to be desired.'

Hot colour flooded her cheeks. That she had asked for the admonition Liz freely admitted. She ought to apologize, she also admitted, but she was suddenly filled with hurt, hurt that gradually overflowed above her anger and desire to say she was sorry. For Nigel to be meeting

Greta after what there was between him and his wife . . . Liz couldn't believe it, even of a Greek. She switched her thoughts, and found herself with the idea that Nigel might just be playing her at her own game. This possibility infuriated her, for it seemed once again to bring him out as the victor.

'You're the last one from whom I should have expected to hear a complaint concerning the manners of anyone else,' she just had to retort, lifting her chin abruptly. 'Up till now your own manners have been pretty appalling!'

He jerked his head, his eyes alight and mocking; her shaft had left him cool and imperturbed as ever.

'That was a childish response, Liz,' he chided gently, his lips twitching as he saw her fists clench again. 'Can't you find something more original than that?' She said nothing, her whole mind being occupied with Greta — and with the picture of her and Nigel together in Athens. 'How soon, I wonder,' Nigel was saying, 'will you lose the habit of retaliation? It's so wearisome . . . and so wasteful of time.'

She twisted her head, aware of the underlying subtlety in both words and tone. Did he mean that, if only she could desist from these thrusts and be feminine and pliable, they could be happy together? If so, it would mean that he loved her. But if he loved her why had he kept away these last few nights? — and why was he intending to see Greta in Athens?

'Are you really going to see Greta?' she blurted out, unable to control the urgency of her heart — and it was her heart that called, she owned freely, looking at him and almost willing him to say no, he wasn't seeing Greta. But he merely scrutinized her for a long moment before he replied, in that lazy drawl which had at first so infuriated her but which, inconsistently, she now found most attractive.

'I've already said that Greta and I shall meet in Athens.' A small pause and then, 'You should be delighted that I'm going away, my dear, for my presence here must surely restrict your activities with your friend Daniel.'

With keen perception she looked at him, her face pale, her lovely eyes dark and yet soft all at once with unconscious pleading.

'You know very well there's nothing between Daniel and me – and never could be.'

'It irks you that I'm not displaying the jealousy you had hoped for?' he queried, lifting his brow.

She said quietly,

'There can be no jealousy without love.'

At his swift agreement portrayed by the quick inclination of his head her mouth quivered. What did she want of this man? Love? Yes, indeed she knew that now. And subservience? – humility? Did she want to override him with her own indefatigable strength of character? Liz shook her head, smiling at her thoughts. Neither man nor woman would ever override Nigel. He was like an ancient warrior, dauntless and imbued with a strength that the most formidable foe could not penetrate. And Liz knew that she would not have him otherwise. She admitted at last that she wanted Nigel just as he was, that if in this partnership there was to be a master, then it must be he.

'You are quite right, Liz, there can be no jealousy without love.' The edge of mocking raillery could not be missed and Liz caught her breath. Was he teasing her? Could it be that he did love her but meant to bring her to her knees before declaring that love? This was too much

162

for Liz, who, forgetful of her thoughts of only a moment ago, lifted her lovely head and sent him a sparkling glance.

'So we thoroughly understand one another. You go to your Greta – and after all, I think I might indulge in an affair with Daniel. As you yourself remarked, we shall both be refreshed by the change!' She rose from her chair and stalked into the house. Behind her, Nigel's soft laugh echoed through the still air, mingling with the shrill chirping of the cicadas. And Liz could have sworn it was a happy laugh – a laugh of triumph and satisfaction.

Despite Nigel's apparent indifference, however, he almost always accompanied Liz and Daniel on their outings. This conduct could of course be merely the courtesy to which a guest was entitled, and yet Liz felt that Nigel did not care a damn for courtesy – at least, not where Daniel was concerned. No, there was another reason why Nigel accompanied them, and Liz began to convince herself that despite his nonchalant attitude Nigel could in fact be jealous.

Previous to Daniel's visit Nigel and Liz had received invitations to a wedding in a small village below Delphi; the preparations went on for two days before the actual ceremony, and guests often took part in these. But Nigel and Liz decided to attend on the day of the ceremony only and of course they took it for granted that Daniel would go with them.

'But I haven't been invited,' he protested instantly. 'No, you two go; I'll enjoy myself around here until you come back.'

Nigel smiled.

'As there will be about five or six hundred guests at this wedding I don't expect another one will make any difference,' he said mildly.

'Five or six hundred?' Daniel stared unbelievingly.

'The whole village is always invited.'

'I couldn't gatecrash, all the same.' Daniel shook his head determinedly.

'The bride's people will be delighted by your appearance. They'd have invited you anyway had you been here at the time they were sending out the invitations. They love to have as many guests as possible at their weddings.'

Daniel could not understand this.

'Surely they think of the expense?'

'They never think of expense at weddings. Besides, it doesn't cost all that much to cater, because the food's prepared by the villagers – if you went today you'd see the bread being baked in the ovens, which are outside the houses. The piglets and the chickens are also cooked outside. No, you needn't worry that your presence will make the slightest difference. There'll be food over, and in plenty. There always is.'

Daniel agreed to go then, but said he had no present to take.

'Then pin some money on the bride's dress,' suggested Nigel.

'Will that be in order?' Daniel gasped, and Nigel smiled and nodded.

'The bride will probably prefer to have the money.'

'Do you know the bride and groom?' asked Daniel curiously as the thought suddenly occurred to him. Both Nigel and Liz shook their heads.

'Never even heard of them.' Nigel laughed at Daniel's expression. 'It's customary for everyone to be invited, and as I said, had you been here when the invitations were sent out you would have received one.'

They set off early the following day, so that Daniel could witness some of the preliminaries going on in the village, the whole of which was a hive of activity with the ovens still working, some sending off delicious smells of newly-baked bread and cakes while from others came the smell of roast chicken or pork.

Outside the bride's house the ceremony of the mattress was going on amid laughter and song and dance. The mattress had already been decorated by the bride's maidens and just as Liz and the two men arrived a baby boy was being bounced gently up and down on it.

'To ensure fertility,' explained Nigel, grinning at his wife.

'Why a boy?' Daniel wanted to know. 'Is there any special significance?'

'Most certainly. The couple will be praying that all their children will be boys, because boys don't require dowries.'

Daniel blinked.

'They still have dowries in Greece?'

'Not only in Greece, but in most Eastern countries.'

'It's incredible!'

'Not at all. It's custom.' Nigel's voice was suddenly crisp. 'The East hasn't progressed as the West—' He spread his hands, his eyes on the mattress on to which people were now throwing coins. This was to ensure that the couple would never be in want. 'But what is progress? One wonders sometimes where progress will eventually lead us.'

A small and rather uncomfortable silence followed this and at length Liz decided to break it.

'I delight in these customs. They savour of such nice simplicity, with all the participants seeming to be so naïve and – and – gentle.' Her voice had smoothed away into a soft musical undertone and, with a sharp twist of his head Nigel looked at her, an odd expression in his eyes.

'The simplicity is very different from what you have been used to,' he murmured, and his words were half statement, half question. Liz lifted her head, and he noticed the dreamy, tranquil expression in her gaze.

'And most refreshing in consequence. I love your customs, Nigel. And your people, who are so sincere and so very hospitable.'

'My people . . .' His voice could be heard, but only just. Liz was left wondering if he would have preferred to be all Greek instead of only 'half and half,' as Grace had once put it.

The mattress was now covered with dainty garments – the bride's trousseau – and then her father appeared, and when the mattress was rolled up he took it on his back and walked into the house with it, followed by the best men – all twenty of them. A short while later they emerged and later still these best men – the *koumbouri* – were watching the bearded priest shaving the bride-groom, out in the garden of his father's house. Meanwhile the bride's maidens were dressing her and making her pretty for the ceremony.

At last the procession was ready. The bride's maidens and many small girls, carrying enormous candles decorated with wide ribbon bows, walked laughingly up to the church. The ceremony began regardless of the clamour going on. A long ribbon was being passed round as the ceremony progressed, and each of the best men signed his name on it. Then snapshots were taken of the bride and groom with the priest smilingly standing between them – smiling because of course a wedding provided a nice little sum for the priest's coffers.

On the return of the procession to the sunlit village the wedding feast began, the tables being laid out in the grounds of the bride's newly-built dowry house.

The three were invited over and over again to stay the night, and could have chosen from at least a dozen hosts, but Nigel smilingly refused.

'We live so close,' he said, but still he was urged to stay. However, at last they drove off, to take the tortuous mountain road up to Kastri. And behind them the whole village shouted and waved, their happy voices mingling with the strains of the *bouzouki* music blaring forth from the laughing band of musicians grouped under a huge tree in the village square.

CHAPTER TEN

WITH the departure of her husband Liz found life more flat than she would ever have believed possible. At home in England she had come to admit that she missed him; here at her home in Greece she missed him even more. What was to become of her? she wondered, looking down from her bedroom window at Daniel, lying on the grass, staring up at the blue sky from behind dark glasses. That Nigel should have gone to Athens surprised her, for he did seem to be watching her, rarely leaving her alone with Daniel. Yet quite carelessly this morning he had said goodbye, those lines at the sides of his eyes fanning out with a sort of mocking amusement because of her expression, which was one of surprise not unmingled with dejection. She knew he would read her mind, but did not care, for the idea of his going to Greta was like a knife twisting in her heart. Liz felt she could not bear it – and instinctively she knew she would not have to should she only lower her pride sufficiently to ask Nigel not to go to Athens.

Pride alone had held her, and now she was sorry. Yet in trying to visualize a scene in which she would ask Nigel to remain here at home she came up against an unfruitful vision. She could never have brought herself to ask him to stay, not under any circumstances. Her pride would not allow it – now or at any other time.

What a situation they were in! If they were ever to make a success of their marriage one of them must inevitably climb down. She herself could not, even in this new and softened mood. Nigel would never do so. It seemed, then, that they were to remain in this position of stalemate all their lives.

With a deep sigh she went down to Daniel. No need to flirt with him any more, and as the day progressed it gradually dawned on him that she was cool now that her husband was not with them and he said perceptively, as they were having dinner that evening,

'It appears it didn't come off.'

She frowned and asked,

'What didn't come off?'

'You were endeavouring to make Nigel jealous. But obviously he's not in the least jealous, otherwise he wouldn't have gone off and left us alone together.'

She felt a rush of anger at his words. More than ever she wished she had not invited him over on this holiday.

'I don't understand you, Daniel. What makes you think I was trying to make Nigel jealous?'

'It was obvious.' He laughed at her expression and added in a rather coaxing tone, 'Don't get mad, Liz. I was only stating a fact; if you're honest you'll admit that you intended using me.' A small pause and then, 'What's wrong? Isn't the marriage going smoothly?'

'You know very well why we married – everyone knew about those wills.'

'Admittedly, but somehow, when I saw you at Grace's a month or two back, I did wonder if you'd married for more than convenience.'

She gave a sigh and said,

'It's something I don't want to talk about, Daniel.'

He shrugged.

'Sorry. We'll change the subject.'

Later Spiros called and Liz sat back for a space and let the two men converse together. But after a while, suddenly realizing that Liz was not participating, Spiros looked apologetically at her and drew her into the conversation.

He stayed till midnight, but at half past eleven Daniel excused himself, saying he could not keep his eyes open.

'It's the enervating climate,' he apologized, and left Spiros and Liz together on the terrace.

'I'm surprised at Nigel's going off like this when you have a guest.' Spiros looked inquiringly at Liz and shook his head.

'I expect he has important business to attend to.' Liz's thoughts flickered to Greta and she caught her lip between her teeth. Visions of Nigel and Greta in Athens spiralling through her mind, she lowered her head to hide her expression. 'He'll be back in a couple of days,' she added, in a sort of endeavour to convince herself that the brevity of the visit would preclude her husband's spending very much time with his girl-friend.

Spiros shrugged in his usual expressive manner, but his eyes became reflective as they peered through the open window to the darkness beyond the immediate half-circle of light sent out by the lamps above the terrace.

'Can't understand,' he murmured to himself, shaking his head. 'Myself—' Bringing his gaze back, Spiros looked bewilderedly at Liz. 'I couldn't leave you, Liz – and certainly I could never have left you here alone with this fellow Daniel.'

She had to smile, because Spiros was reddening swiftly, aware of his lack of tact. She did not spare him as she said,

'You would not trust me?'

'I'm one big fool, as I've said before. Of course I'd trust you.'

'Then why wouldn't you leave me here with Daniel?'

she asked softly.

'I just couldn't leave you at all. My God, Liz, can't he see how lovely you are?' Spiros was becoming heated and Liz's eyes widened. Not complications with Spiros, she hoped. There could be, should it ever occur to him that Nigel did not love her.

'Nigel must attend to his business,' she said unemotionally. 'He can't neglect it simply because he's married.'

'But you could go with him. He used to take—' Again Spiros broke off, his colour increasing.

'Greta?' she finished, wincing even as she uttered the name.

'Yes, Greta. You know about her, so there's no point in trying to get myself out of the muddle I'm in,' he answered resignedly. 'And I might as well tell you, Liz, that the whole thing's a great puzzle to me—'

'You've just implied that, Spiros.'

'And if I didn't know Greta happens to be here in Delphi,' he went on as if Liz had never interrupted, 'I'd be very much inclined to believe she was with him.'

Liz stared wordlessly at him, and a long silence ensued. Spiros opened his mouth at last, intending to apologize but Liz was before him.

'Greta is here . . . in Delphi?'

'That's right.' He stopped, eyeing her in some puzzlement. 'Liz—!' he exclaimed perceptively. 'Liz, you didn't think—? No, you must not! I told you before, Nigel would never let you down. You didn't think he was with Greta – you couldn't!'

A slow triumphant smile was curving her lips. Yet she had to say,

'You seem to have a very short memory, Spiros. You yourself have just a moment ago said that, had Greta not been here in Delphi, you'd be very much inclined to believe she was with Nigel in Athens.'

'I did say that, yes, but I didn't mean it.' He spoke with a certain awkwardness and Liz decided to allow the matter to drop, her mind in any case being occupied with the news Spiros had just imparted, and in this moment of discovery she wondered how Nigel could have made the miscalculation of being so sure of her not discovering the truth. That he had been playing her at her own game was certain, but this time he hadn't been at all successful. Wait until he returned . . . Would she tell him what she knew, though? It might be more entertaining to keep quiet.

He was back before lunch and Liz calculated that he must have started from Athens very early indeed. He had been away only a day and a half, but two nights. She subjected him to a long and rather amused scrutiny when on coming on to the verandah, he greeted her cordially and immediately asked if she were enjoying herself with Daniel.

'Very much.' She continued to scrutinize him. 'Did you enjoy yourself with Greta?' she inquired sweetly.

He nodded.

'It was most diverting.'

She smiled at him.

'And you've returned – er – refreshed?'

'Absolutely.' He sent her a slanting glance of amusement, tinged as usual with satire. 'And you,' he drawled, 'are you refreshed?' He was laughing at her. She was tempted to let him know that she also could laugh – at his expense. But that would bring down the curtain on this delightful little farce, and such was Liz's enjoyment that she only wished to prolong it.

'So-so . . . I could have done with your staying away

a little longer, though.'

Nigel laughed, and with a lightning movement he had her in his arms.

'You wretch, Liz – you delectable wretch! I shall be driven to beating you in the end. In fact, I'm inclined to think I should have done it long ago.' Instead, he kissed her, in a way that left her breathless, and she took in gulps of air while Nigel still held her, firmly, and looked down at her, with considerable amusement. 'Did you miss me?' he asked suddenly and unexpectedly. Liz lifted her head, but he gave her no opportunity of voicing the retort which flashed to her lips. 'I'll not allow you to lie,' he said, and pressed his mouth to hers again. 'You did miss me – and always will whenever I'm away. Admit it—' He gave her a little shake. 'Drop that damned armour and admit it!'

'I certainly missed the arguments,' she replied in honeyed tones. 'And your pompous, self-opinionated comments. It's been wonderfully peaceful and, as I've just said, I could have done with your staying away a little while longer.'

'Liar!'

'I'm not!'

He held her arms, but pushed her away from him, his regard searching and accusing.

'You're not, eh?' His voice was soft, his dark eyes still holding hers in a steadfast gaze until at length she was obliged to lower her head. 'Well, in that case you'll not mind if I return to Athens. In fact, I came back merely for some papers I'd forgotten.' Slow and stressed the words, and his eyes still searched. With a careless finger under her chin he forced her to meet his gaze. 'I'll be back a couple of days before we go to Rhodes.'

Her heart seemed to sink right into her feet. Why was

she so stupid? Still, she could not have kept him, it seemed — not if he spoke the truth when he said he'd returned only to pick up some papers he had forgotten. Releasing her, he moved away, going into the room to pour himself a drink. Was he speaking the truth? From what she knew of him he was thorough, and methodical. So it was unlikely he had forgotten vital documents. These would be the first things of which he would think, and accordingly they would have been put into his brief-case. The more she considered this the more she began to suspect that pique alone had forced him to say he was going away again. Surely, though, he would not go — not if there was nothing to go for, which Liz suspected was the case. He returned to the verandah, a glass in his hand.

'When are you returning to Athens?' she asked, her spirits still greatly dampened by reason of her own obsti-nacy and deliberate refusal to give an inch.

'Later this afternoon.' He appeared bored all at once and as Daniel had come down from taking a shower and was now in the garden Liz left her husband ... but her footsteps dragged a little and behind her Nigel allowed himself a very satisfied smile.

The fact that he had not been with Greta was sufficient evidence that Nigel was playing Liz at her own game, and in all fairness she could not blame him. Also, he was not in the least troubled by her hints regarding her relation-ship with Daniel. She might just as well have saved her breath, she concluded, for he knew exactly what she was about. By now, however, the game they were both en-gaged in was fast becoming irksome. That she loved her husband she freely owned. That she wanted him just as he was she also freely admitted. And in addition she had a shrewd suspicion that Grace had been right when she suggested that Nigel had married Liz because he loved her. In fact, that could be the only reason – Liz saw that now. For otherwise he would not have left her like this. No, the reason for his leaving her was to bring her round, she felt sure. And if that were the case he knew his love was returned. She went out to Daniel, heaving a deep sigh as she swung off the patio and walked towards him. The only problem appeared to be that of capitulation – whole and complete surrender on her part. Nigel would accept nothing less and he meant to continue the wearing-down process until his desire was fulfilled, no matter what it cost him. Liz's mouth compressed at this idea. She was no stupid fawning female ready to supplicate herself before a mere male! No, she would see him in Hades first!

They flew to Rhodes, gliding over the shimmering Aegean with its numerous islands, scattered like gems gleaming in the sunshine. Nigel spoke little on the flight and Liz sat in thoughtful silence, looking down and wondering that her home in England, loved for so long, and for which she had sacrificed her life – or so she had believed at the time of her marriage – should have receded into the misty backcloth of her mind, replaced by Nigel's lovely villa, so small by comparison to Carlington Hall, standing proudly on its plateau on the mountainside, surrounded by tropical trees and shrubs, and looking out on to the towering massif of Parnassus and the great Plain of Amphissa with its silver sea of olives.

From the airport they drove by taxi to the harbour at Mandraki, where the great yacht was moored. Many other yachts and pleasure craft were there, with people moving about on them or just lazing around. On a few of the vessels workmen were busy – brown-faced workmen,

Greeks employed by the wealthy owners of the boats.

The new experience was exciting to Liz and she was very different from the one-time proud mistress of Carlington Hall as she exclaimed repeatedly on being shown over the yacht.

'It's really magnificent,' she said later when she and Nigel were in their cabin preparing for dinner. The idea of the one cabin pleased her; it forced her husband's hand, as it were, for since that night when he had so abruptly left her he had never been to her room. All the way out she had wondered about the accommodation, and nothing would have been more disappointing than to find that they had been allotted two separate cabins. She should have known, though, for even dismissing the fact of the question of the limited space on a vessel like this, no Greek would think of separating husband and wife.

'You're quite enamoured with it, aren't you?' Cool the tone, but Nigel smiled at her all the same. 'Perhaps I'll consider having a vessel like this. We could sail to all the islands.'

Her eyes glowed.

'I'd like that.' Automatically she turned her back to him and he brought up her zip-fastener. His hands remained on her, moving to her neck and then to her throat. He turned her round to face him.

'You're very beautiful, my Liz.' His eyes were tender and Liz knew instinctively that she only had to nestle close to him, and it would all be over – the struggles of them both. And yet she could not, because such an action would savour of surrender and she felt sure Nigel would produce that mocking satirical smile and that it would also hold triumph, triumph in no small degree. And so she stood there, a little stiff because of her determination to hold fast to her vow never to be conquered. Nigel gave a tiny sigh and, kissing her lightly on the cheek, he turned away and went to a drawer, looking for a handkerchief.

There were ten other people on board, among whom were Annette and Claire, and their husbands. The two girls were glad to see Liz again and after Liz had been introduced to all the others she and the two English girls, finding themselves together in the salon when the pre-dinner drinks were being served, became engrossed in conversation. It was while being similarly engaged in conversation like this with Annette and Claire that she had experienced that first fleeting dart of jealousy against Greta, Liz recalled, her eyes straying, now as then, to her husband. And as before he stood by the cocktail bar, deep in conversation with several of his Greek friends. After a while, sensing her interest, he turned his head and his dark eyes flickered over her. Liz was reminded of that other impact as, her lips forming a ready smile, she experienced a similar impact, but this time it was much stronger than on that first occasion.

After dinner several couples left the boat, to stroll on the waterfront, or to find entertainment. Nigel and Liz went off together, on their own.

They strolled up out of the New Town and entered a romantic park laid out by the tree and flower-loving Italians when they were in occupation. Gigantic date palms were surrounded by smaller palms; there were rhododendron bushes and hibiscus, and shady walks where shadows moved as the tropical vegetation was gently swayed by the *Meltemi* breaking on to the shore.

'There's the castle,' commented Nigel, pointing, and Liz glanced up. The park was coming to an abrupt end and the massive pinnacles and towers, hewn from honey-coloured weathered limestone, loomed ahead of her. Massive gates guarded the fortress of the Knights of the ancient Order of St. John of Jerusalem, among whose members had been a great many of the famous Crusaders. As they neared the fortress, lights were switched on, softly enhancing the delicate patina of age which hung over the whole delightful edifice. Nigel said,

'The *son et lumière* spectacle's about to begin. Would you like to hear it?' And when she nodded eagerly, 'We'll have to see what language it's in. English, French or Greek will do us?' He smiled as he waited for her answer, which was as he expected.

'If it's in Greek you'll have the task of translating it for me.'

'Which will be a pleasure,' he returned gallantly, and Liz was glad of the shadows because of her blushes and the softness that entered her eyes.

The language that night happened to be English, and, with his arm under hers in a distinctly proprietorial way, Nigel led her over to the hut where a smiling Greek waited to accept their money.

In the grounds of the castle people strolled about, for the spectacle was not due to begin for another fifteen minutes. Everywhere were trees and flowers – palms and pines, swathed against the velvet of a moon-flushed sky, hibiscus and roses and poinsettias growing in profusion. The muted voices of the pedestrians mingled with the shrill chirping of crickets in the olive trees' trembling foliage. Liz became wrapped in meditation, thinking of the vicissitudes through which the lovely island had passed – from the time of Antigonus, son of Alexander the Great, who laid siege to the city of Rhodes, right down the ages of history from the Roman occupation through the Byzantine era, which included the period of occupation by the famous Knights Crusaders. Then the Knights were attacked and defeated by the Turks under

Suleiman the Magnificent, after which came the Italians – tree-planters who gave Rhodes its glorious parks and tree-lined roads and shady squares. And now Rhodes was free, part of the motherland of Greece.

The silence between Liz and Nigel was intimate and profound, like the gentle hush of night, when all nature sleeps and the lull of conflict seems redolent of the peace of heaven itself. Liz glanced sideways and upwards, her eyes limpid and tender. Her heart jerked at the magnificence of her husband. Head and shoulders above her – and in fact above everyone else, it seemed – he moved with the easy grace of something aided by wings. So light, he appeared, and yet strength could be sensed even in his movements and the way he swung his arm. The other arm was still under her elbow, but as they turned to retrace their steps towards the courtyard where the chairs were arrayed in a semi-circle ready for the spectacle, he pulled her arm through his and held it close. She felt his warmth and swallowed saliva collecting in her mouth. Why should she hold out when she wanted him so much? It was ridiculous, and Liz was ready to admit it. If only she were ready to capitulate ... Or if Nigel would make the first move instead of remaining so inflexible and determined to play his waiting game.

They sat down, watching the lights, radiant and lustrous, playing at first on one part of the castle and then on another, their shades ranging from deep bronze through to pale gold and from deepest crimson through to soft and shell-like pink.

Then the voices came, loud and clear – voices from a distant glorious past. The knights in conference ... Here the lights moved to a room high in the castle and it was the easiest thing in the world actually to *see* that conference.

'What a wonderful thing the imagination is,' Liz breathed, her dreamy gaze high on the windows of that turreted room. Nigel nodded.

'This sound and light is always most effective. I always thoroughly enjoy it. I went to the acropolis in Athens the other evening . . .' He tailed off. Not like him, she mused, smiling secretly. Yet she had to say, in a spirit of pure mischief,

'With Greta?'

Silence. Had her tone given her away? she wondered. No, it hadn't – and Liz could not have said whether she was glad or sorry.

'Need we spoil this evening?' he asked, crisp-voiced, and Liz swallowed hard.

'I'm sorry.' The apology was out, surprising them both, but a swift jerk of Nigel's head was the only evidence he gave of this surprise and once again they lapsed into silence, listening to the voices reaching them from out of the long ago. The Great Magistrate, Villiers de l'Isle Adam, rallying his armies and bidding them hold out, for the siege of the Sultan could not endure. Then the voice of Suleiman, discouraged and ready to call off his armies. The lights moved to another room high on a tower. The two officers of the Knights and the Albanian traitor talking to Suleiman, telling him of the weakness of the defenders. The finale was wonderful but sad, for the gallant Knights, forced to surrender, raised a white flag at the gate of St. John, and as the final scene faded they were mournfully leaving the island to the victorious Turks, who were to occupy it for nearly four hundred years.

Liz sat there for a few moments after the spectacle was finished, even though others were moving.

'It was marvellous, but sad,' she said, and the small lines at the sides of Nigel's face fanned out as he glanced at her in some amusement.

'You knew it was going to be a sad ending.' She merely nodded and Nigel went on, in a very quiet tone, 'You don't care for sad endings, apparently?'

'One has to be realistic. Most endings are sad – if one carries a story on long enough.'

'Not all, my dear.' He did not go on to explain that, but standing up, he waited for her to do likewise and then, taking her arm, he walked with her towards the gate through which they had entered about an hour ago.

On returning to the yacht they found that only Dendras and his wife were on board, all the others having gone off either dancing or to hotels to drink and watch the cabaret.

'This is a nice sort of party,' Liz whispered to Nigel. 'We can all do exactly what we want to do without worrying about offending our hosts.'

Nigel nodded, and for a while the four sat on deck talking and watching the lights in the harbour, lights from the boats as well as those along the waterfront.

It was almost midnight when the rest of the party returned, and as the night was still warm they all remained on deck for another hour or so before saying good night and going to their respective cabins.

Once inside theirs Liz smiled at her husband. She was exultant because of the situation in which they found themselves. Nigel would have to stay with her, because he had no alternative, and she had made up her mind to let him see that she loved him. He would then make the first move and she would be satisfied. It did strike her that she was being rather inconsistent in wanting Nigel to humble himself, as it were, for she had already decided she preferred him just as he was. However, she dismissed the matter of her inconsistency and gave him another swift smile. To her surprise Nigel seemed unaware of it, for he turned from her and stood by the porthole, looking out to the shapeless dark mass of the sea.

'It's a lovely night,' he remarked at length, turning his head. 'I think I'll sleep on deck.'

On deck ... Liz swallowed something hard in her throat. She heard herself say,

'You'll not be very comfortable.'

'Those deck-chairs are as good as beds.' His voice was cool, expressionless, his gaze indifferent.

She looked down at her hands, conscious of the emptiness within her. Had she made a mistake? Could it be that Nigel did not want her – not now?

'It'll be cold – later, and – and damp.'

'There are sleeping bags in a cupboard on deck. Dendras always keeps a good supply in case anyone wants to sleep outside.'

He had been gone twenty minutes or so and Liz was still sitting there, on a chair, her mind perceptive, yet wavering between resignation and obstinacy. Nigel loved her, she felt convinced of this, but love would never humble him. If she wanted him she must go to him.

Another ten minutes elapsed and to her astonishment she realized her eyes were filmed over, reflecting the hurt that dragged at her heart.

She began to undress, determined not to capitulate. And the next moment she was admitting that, whatever she did tonight, it would be only a temporary thing; tomorrow night this would happen again. And so it would continue until one of them gave way— No, until she gave way.

'I won't! He'll get tired before I!' And even though she was quite convinced that he never would get tired Liz finished undressing and got into bed.

An hour later, having tossed and turned incessantly as sleep eluded her, Liz rose from the bed and slipped into a warm housecoat. But it took a great deal of determination – and time – for her to make up her mind. Once she had made it up, though, she never wavered. Life could not go on like this.

He stood by the rail and, surprised, she glanced around, looking for the chair, and the sleeping bag he had mentioned. There was no sign of them and she moved closer, noticing his stillness and apparent concentration on the lights of the boats in the harbour and along the waterfront. Cafés and hotels were still brilliantly lighted and people strolled about, or occupied the little flower-shaded recesses that ran all along the front of the harbour.

Another step and she halted; he had sensed her presence and she saw his head come round, and then his whole body.

It was a profound moment, as they stood there, in that balmy Eastern atmosphere, staring at one another, a moment of rarity and indescribable sweetness.

And then Nigel suddenly shattered the spell by his prosaic question.

'What is it, Liz?'

She took another step towards him.

'I couldn't sleep,' she answered softly, keeping her head averted because should she encounter a gloating, triumphant expression on his face all her good resolutions might just be thrown to the winds.

'That's not like you, is it?' Wordlessly she shook her head. 'Can I get you a nightcap?'

She winced. What was he trying to do? Perhaps he did not love her after all . . . She shook her head as an echo of memory brought back his advice to her, his advice to keep on guessing and she might eventually hit upon the truth. She ignored his question.

'I've been thinking,' she murmured in accents soft and persuasive, and Nigel moved so that he could reach out and tilt her chin.

'What about?' His eyes searched hers; she managed an indeterminate smile, and saw in the half light that his expression had taken on a hint of censure. Her smile straightened then, yet still she hovered between complete acceptance of her fate and the last remaining spark of resistance.

'About what you once said. You told me to keep on guessing.'

A small silence, broken by laughter from the shore.

'I believe I did.' He was chary, she noticed; not a trace of mockery or taunting amusement. 'And have you been guessing, Liz?'

She nodded, automatically touching his hand which was still holding her chin. Nigel curled his fingers round it, and held it to his breast.

'You said I might guess why you married me.' And when he made no comment, 'I think you married me because – because . . .' She tailed off, fear taking possession for a space. But as she looked into his features she saw in the glimmer of light that they had softened, and his gaze was infinitely tender. 'Was it because you loved me?' she continued, confident yet faintly pleading.

For answer he drew her to him, and held her so close that she actually felt the great trembling sigh that escaped from the very heart of him. Only then did she realize that he had almost given up hope.

'Yes, Liz, I married you because I loved you.' He paused a moment, listening to the sough of the breeze as it swept the rippling waves. 'Do I take it that my love is returned?' he whispered close to her cheek.

184

'I love you,' she responded simply, and with that admission the last of her adamance transmuted to a sweet and gentle surrender as she lifted her face, inviting his kiss.

For a long while there was silence between them and then, clearly all confidence again, Nigel asked her why it had taken her so long to come out to him.

'You were expecting me?' she asked, and when he nodded, and those little lines fanned out, a sparkle should by rights have entered Liz's eyes, but they were dreamy and cloudy from his lovemaking, and in any case she did not mind at all that he had expected her to come to him. It all seemed as it should be, somehow.

'But as the time passed,' Nigel was saying, 'I became half afraid you'd wrap that armoured cloak more tightly around you and, protected by it, fall into a contented sleep.'

She had to laugh.

'And you'd have done it all for nothing.'

'I'd have kept on trying.' But he frowned and once again Liz felt he had just about come to the end of his tether and she drew close to him, just to demonstrate her love. He found her lips again, kissing her with tender yet ardent emotion.

'Darling,' he whispered close to her face, 'I wasn't with Greta last week.'

She hesitated, but the demands of honesty brought forth the words,

'I knew you weren't. She was in Delphi.'

He held her away, looking at her.

'How did you discover that?'

'It's all right, she didn't visit me again, if that's what you're thinking. Spiros told me.'

His mouth tightened slightly.

'Spiros is altogether too darned interfering. And you,' he added as the thought occurred to him, 'you knew all the time, then?'

She nodded.

'Yes, I knew.'

'And yet you let me go on saying I'd enjoyed myself—'

'And refreshed yourself,' she just had to remind him, and received a little shake for her trouble.

'Laughing at me, eh?'

'Well, Nigel, if I was you did ask for it. And besides, you've been laughing at me from the very first.'

At the little plaintive note his spark of anger flickered out.

'In future, my darling, we'll laugh together, not at each other.'

She nodded dreamily and rested her head against him. But in a little while she murmured,

'Up there in the *khani* – I think you nearly told me you loved me.'

'I did,' he admitted and, anticipating her question, 'I had second thoughts because I somehow felt you weren't quite ready to receive a declaration of love – not in the way I wanted you to receive it.'

'I wasn't humble enough?' The inevitable sparkle in her voice, which melted the instant she saw his expression.

'I never wanted you to be humble, Liz. Nor do I desire it now. But I did want a woman for a wife – a woman with all the endearing attributes that appeal to a man.' He shook his head in a gesture of admonition. 'You were an idiot, Liz!'

She nodded an agreement and as the thought came to her she asked Nigel what he had meant when he asserted that Spiros didn't know what he was talking about.

'He thought he knew what he was talking about,' Nigel answered reflectively. 'He told you of my intention of contesting the wills. But what knowledge he had was no longer relevant, because I fell in love with you the moment I kissed you in that tent.'

'But Spiros didn't know anything about my being connected with the will.'

'That's just it. He rambled on, and all he did was to upset you – unknowingly, it was true, but he did upset you nevertheless, and that was why I was so furious.'

'I understand now.' She was silent for a moment. 'Nigel . . .'

'Sweetheart?'

'You didn't really want to have an affair with Greta, did you?'

Silence. Liz wondered if she had utterly ruined this lovely situation. But after a while Nigel said, though rather stiffly.

'What makes you say a thing like that?'

'It was because of what you said about the strongest of us succumbing to temptation. I took it that she – Greta – was so attractive that you just – well – fell for her, even though you didn't really want to.'

He looked at Liz, shaking his head in a little gesture of exasperation.

'If you had thought about that statement, my love, you would have made another correct guess. I referred to the temptation which you yourself put in my way. I saw you and was lost.'

She stared unbelievingly.

'So it had nothing to do with Greta?' Liz recalled her own sense of optimism, when she had thought that if Nigel had not really wanted to fall for Greta in the first place then there was hope for her, Liz. 'Aren't I silly?' she murmured, speaking her thoughts aloud.

'I'm afraid I must agree, heartily!'

She looked up and laughed and after an intimate moment or two Nigel held her away from him again and said, without much expression,

'Greta and her parents are leaving Delphi. Her father's bought a small fruit farm on the island of Samothrace – which is in the far north of Greece,' he added, 'a very long way from Delphi.' Nigel looked down at his wife, who made no comment on what he had just said. 'I love you, Liz,' he told her tenderly. 'I want you to know, my darling, that you're the only woman I've ever loved ... or ever will love. Do you understand what I say?'

She smiled happily, and would have spoken, but Nigel's kiss prevented speech, and so she gave herself up to the bliss of the moment before, pulling her arm through his, Nigel guided her to the steps which led down to their cabin.

Other titles available this month in the Mills & Boon Classics Series

3 specially chosen reissues of the best in Romantic Fiction

THE NIGHT OF THE HURRICANE
by Andrea Blake

Julie's idyllic life on a lonely Caribbean island ended when her father remarried and her stepmother tried to persuade him to sell the place. Even after her marriage to Simon Tiernan, Julie felt her stepmother's malicious influence.

MASK OF SCARS
by Anne Mather

Christina's brother was running a hotel in the Algarve, in southern Portugal, so when her long vacation came along, it struck her as a good idea to go and spend it with him. At any rate, it seemed a good idea until she realised just how unwelcome she was! Nevertheless, she soon began to wonder if she had done the right thing when she took the job offered her by the local lord of the manor ...

A MAN OF AFFAIRS
(The Widening Stream)
by Rachel Lindsay

When Melanie Powell became engaged to an American, she invited her friend Loris Cameron to accompany her on a visit to his family home in California, and on the way Loris too fell in love — with Brett Halliday. But both girls were to have a long way to travel before they reached the end of their journey to happiness.

Mills & Boon Classics
— all that's great in Romantic Reading!

Available November 1979

Mills & Boon Classics

The very best of Mills and Boon
romances, brought back for those
of you who missed reading them
when they were first published.

and in
December
we bring back the following four
great romantic titles.

THE TIME OF THE JACARANDA *by Margaret Way*
Grant Manning, the owner of the beautiful Australian station
of Saranga, was a man to contend with. Adrienne saw the
station as a means of escape — but how could she escape
Grant?

THE SILVER SLAVE *by Violet Winspear*
The imposing Dom Duarte de Montqueiro Ardo thought that
Rosary was too young and inexperienced to tutor his
daughter. And that wasn't the only problem . . .

TANGLE IN SUNSHINE *by Rosalind Brett*
Tessa instantly resented David Clavering, but as she grew to
know him better, she found herself hoping that he might not
be too deeply attracted to her cousin Raine.

LEGACY OF THE PAST *by Anne Mather*
The only two men in Madeline's life so far had been gentle
and kind. Nicholas Vitale was anything but gentle — but
Madeline couldn't resist him . . .

You can obtain all these titles from your local paperback retailer.
If you have any difficulty in obtaining any of them through your local
shop, write to:

Mills and Boon Reader Service,
P.O. Box No 236, Thornton Road, Croydon, Surrey CR9 3RU.